WITCH SISTERS

WITCH SISTERS

Alanna Murphy

ISBN: 978-1-78324-127-9

Published by Wordzworth
www.wordzworth.com

CONTENTS

HERE

CHAPTER 1

HOME

It was 1:30 P.M. and Kaj was still sleeping, which was not surprising. Kaj never woke up early, especially after a night of witchcraft. I walked upstairs and quietly opened Kaj's door. Framboise stretched and purred as I said good morning to the little cat.

"Wake up, Kaj! It's after 1 in the afternoon."

Kaj groaned and pulled the covers a little higher over her head. Kaj's room was littered with wine glasses still containing remnants of the cabernet we were drinking the previous evening. Her tarot cards were scattered over the wooden floor, there were numerous matchboxes dispersed on top of her cabinet, and there was incense ash and candle wax dripping from the window sill.

"Your room is a mess," I told her, as if she didn't know it already.

"What time are we leaving?" grumbled Kaj from under her covers.

"As soon as you wake up!"

I walked downstairs with the hopes that Kaj would get moving. We were all going out for the day to pick up some magical herbs and potions. Every so often, we needed to replenish our supplies so that we could properly practice our powers.

As Kaj got up and started getting ready, Topaz sat out in the garden meditating with her crystals. The sun was bright but some storm clouds could be seen out in the distance. Topaz stared up at the ball of fire in the sky. She had a habit of staring at the sun. She claimed it gave her energy.

Bayou walked over to Topaz. Topaz got startled when Bayou popped up behind her.

"Oh, Bayou! You scared me!"

"Really? I thought you saw me coming," Bayou said. "What are you doing? Are we still going today?"

"I think so. Is Kaj up yet?"

"Yea, she's just getting out of the shower. I saw her in the bathroom putting jojoba oil on her face."

"Ok, I guess I'll go upstairs and start to get ready too."

Topaz picked up her bowl of crystals and headed back inside to prepare for the day ahead. She stared up at the sun one last time before closing the patio door.

While Kaj and Topaz finished getting ready, I decided to sit and read a little. I opened "Jitterbug Perfume," a Tom Robbins book I acquired from Topaz's mystical book collection. Topaz's room is like a strange, mind-bending library. I know I can always find something interesting to read in there. Meanwhile, Bayou did some headstands outside to get the

4

blood rushing to her head. Bayou is always twisting, turning, cracking, and popping her body into different positions so that she can fully absorb the divine energies.

Finally, all four of us met up in the kitchen, ready for a fun adventure to our favorite little shop.

CHAPTER 2

AELLA, BAYOU, TOPAZ, AND KAJ

Before we go too far, let me acquaint you with the witch sisters. Us witch sisters are no ordinary sisters. In fact, we are quite strange siblings. Well, at least that's what all those basic witches out there think (I call them basic witches because in reality, ALL females are witches. It's just that the basic ones don't know it yet, or worse, deny it). But let's be real, we couldn't care less what those other "normal" people think. At least not anymore. Maybe there was a time, a long time ago, when we wanted to fit in. But that was back before we knew how powerful we were.

My name is Aella, and my three sorcerous sisters are named Bayou, Topaz, and Kaj. We each have our own unique set of powers, which we can choose to use for either the good, or the bad, of the Universe. Each of our powers are related to our elements- air, water, fire, and earth. Besides our unique gifts, we all share certain practical powers. For example, all of us have the ability to communicate with animals, and we each have our own pets which are here to guide us along on our journeys. We also have the ability to make men fall madly in love with us, or make men scared as hell of us. Unfortunately, we often have trouble controlling which of the two will happen.

The four of us live in a palace on a lake surrounded by a thriving garden. We live there with our mom and dad, along with our three cats, my macaw, Bayou's red-eared slider turtle, Topaz's lizard/dragon and Kaj's earthworm. In addition, we have numerous bunnies hopping around our garden, a couple of iguanas that live out in the trees, some spiders that weave their way in and around the house, and birds that come around regularly for free peanuts. We also have a young crow that our father, Murf, found injured during a storm and nursed back to life. Rocky the crow protects and brings omens to the family. We grew up in a safe, loving, creative home. The palace is the perfect place for us to practice our craft without interference from the outside world. However, we don't really like to practice when our parents are around. While mom and dad hear us talking about other dimensions, powerful plants, space travel, and elves, they think we are just playing around. They don't *actually* believe they created four witches. Little do they know.

I, Aella, am the oldest of the four witch sisters. My element, air, gives me the power to travel through space and time. I can visit the past and the future through dreams and visions. However, much of my dreams are dark and blurry, making it difficult to cipher through them. Kaj tells me that my scorpio moon accounts for my dark dreams and inner emotions. One of my biggest passions is traveling. I love traveling, not only through space and time, but also in real life. Taking trips to exotic places on earth, as well as traveling to unseen dimensions, excites me like nothing else! I seek adventure and am very much a free-spirit. I love meeting interesting individuals and going places I've never been. I prefer to travel alone, but I know the importance of traveling with others too, especially with my sisters. I truly believe that trips open up your world to magic, and that's what life is about. My macaw, Soleil, will sometimes accompany me on my journeys. Soleil and I have a serious connection. We definitely knew each other in a past life. Soleil can be feisty and even aggressive towards others, especially males, but it's only because she is extremely protective. Soleil watches over the palace and makes sure no intruders try to sneak in and around the property. She'll squawk bloody murder as soon as she sees something suspicious. While I am a free-spirit, I am also the responsible sister. I am generally the one who plans and organizes amongst the girls. I am pretty good at balancing life's chaotic twists and turns while still enjoying the ride and laughing at the irony of it all.

Bayou, the second sister, is a water witch. Because her element is water, she is highly sensitive. She has the ability to feel energies. Bayou is always doing yoga and finds that yoga enhances her connection to herself and others. She is very attached to her home and has a natural "mother" energy. She loves and understands children and often uses her powers to influence them in positive ways. Bayou also appreciates her sleep. During her sleeping hours, she finds time to heal her body and her mind while getting in touch with important messages sent from the source. Bayou has a little turtle that lives out in the lake. She raised him from the time he was just a tiny creature and released him in the lake when he was big enough to survive on his own. Her turtle often comes out from the lake to visit Bayou and give her messages and words of wisdom. Bayou likes to spend time out in the garden with her precious turtle along with all the rabbits who seem to multiply faster than Bayou can keep up with. She loves bunnies and often dreams about them. Bayou has a special psychic ability to see things before they happen. Sometimes she will get a strange feeling about someone or something. She never hides her emotions so we always know what is on Bayou's mind. Bayou is extremely compassionate and has the ability to empathize with the pain and suffering of all the various souls of the world.

Topaz is as much a witch as she is a shaman. Her element is fire, which suits her perfectly. Though she is the quietest of all the girls, she has a fiery passion that intimidates many. Her unique power is her ability to connect to the spirit realm. Topaz spends a lot of time by herself, reading and meditating. She doesn't care much for people. She'd rather be alone with her crystals and her books, practicing her powers, and tapping into other unseen worlds. Topaz is extremely knowledgeable about various plant medicines and their enlightening abilities. She often administers ceremonies to us witch sisters using some of her favorite earthly concoctions, hence, her nickname "the sexy shaman." Topaz has a lizard/dragon named Blaise as her trusty sidekick. Her primitive pet resembles an iguana in this world, but as soon as he enters other dimensions, Blaise becomes his higher self, aka a fire-breathing beast. Topaz is very focused and driven, but only when it comes to her interests. If something isn't of importance to her, she won't give it any attention. Topaz loves dark chocolate and often has chocolate smeared on her face or in her hair and doesn't even realize it. She spends more time in the spirit realm than she does in the "real world," which gives her the unique ability to understand things many will just never comprehend.

Kaj is the youngest of the four. She is extremely witty, and definitely the most animated of the girls. Her element, earth, allows her to heal people and animals through her use of concoctions she whips up using herbs, spices, flowers, and whatever other random stuff she finds. She is always mixing up natural elements to create soaps, lotions, teas, soups and stews. She loves beautiful things and often collects pretty little pieces of art or jewelry to create a magical space for all of us girls to practice our powers. Kaj is a party. She likes to stay up late into the dark hours of the night, sometimes getting herself into trouble. She has a deep appreciation for music and movies. She plays the role of the DJ when all of us are together, introducing us to obscure sounds that the average person probably wouldn't even recognize as music. She carries her tarot cards with her at all times, allowing her to give readings to us as well as to strangers. Kaj became really good friends with a little worm that lives in the palace garden. They met on a rainy day when Kaj was out in the yard plucking some aloe vera. Kaj almost accidentally stepped on the earthworm with her bare feet as her toes dug into the moist soil.

"Oh dear, I almost stepped on you little buddy" exclaimed Kaj as she lifted her new friend out of the dirt. Kaj and Sam (the earthworm) immediately became friends when Sam found out Kaj was vegan (as are all the witch sisters). Sam is gender fluid (earth worms are both male and female) and Sam sometimes gets confused as he/she doesn't realize that not *all* creatures are hermaphrodites. When Kaj isn't sleeping the day away, she can often be found out in the garden with Sam, humming a tune while watering, plucking, digging and planting. Kaj is also quite adept in astrology and can find out all kinds of secrets about people by consulting the stars. We usually go to her when we need to dig up some dirt on our latest crushes.

While each of us is powerful on our own, together, we form a union that is more dynamic and potent than anything this planet has seen in a long, long time...

CHAPTER 3

_____

SIMON'S SORCERY SHOP

The sky was baby blue and there were a few wispy white clouds scattered around the lower half of the horizon. A slight breeze made the temperature feel just right. As we arrived at our supply store, we noted how beautiful it was outside. There were some birds chirping in the distance, butterflies fluttering around the flowers lining the shop, and the wind was whispering hidden messages to those that chose to listen. We walked up the stone pathway that led to the entrance and opened the door of our favorite shop. Simon was expecting us to arrive today and he was delighted when we showed up.

"Simon!!!" we all exclaimed in unison.

"AHHH!! How are you girls?!" Simon ran over and lifted us up one by one in his customary embrace. "Oh my god. It has been so crazy today. You girls came at the perfect time because this morning was insane."

Simon went on to tell us about all the obnoxious characters he had to deal with earlier that day. We were all laughing
hysterically as Simon impersonated the old woman who
tried to shoplift a pendulum and started crying when she got
caught. "You girls have no idea what I have to deal with on
a daily basis."

"Oh, I can only imagine," Kaj replied, laughing and rolling
her eyes.

I looked around the shop and noticed all kinds of new
stuff. Simon was always replenishing his supplies and finding
new, cool, beautiful items to add to his shop's collection. I
could smell the palo santo incense burning and I glanced the
shelves to find magical crystals, intricately carved totems, and
various decks of tarot cards. Dream weavers hung from the
ceiling and lit candles gave the shop a spooky glow.

"I am always so impressed at your ever-changing collection," I told Simon.

"This is nothing. Are you girls ready to see what I've got
for YOU?" Simon winked and led the four of us into the back
room.

Behind the wall of loose-leaf teas is a sliding door that
leads to where all the good stuff hides. "I've been working on
some special potions lately and I think you guys will like what
I've got." The back room was like a trippy candy store. There
were all kinds of exotic plants and herbs lying between pots
and pans bubbling with strange concoctions. Simon picked
up a bag of dried something or other and handed it to Topaz.
"You will definitely be wanting this." He then grabbed a few
different glass bottles from the wooden shelf and examined

them, trying to remember what was in them. He shrugged and handed them to us anyways. "Oooh, Bayou, I got this lemongrass mist I've been wanting to give you!" Simon handed Bayou the fresh mist and she thanked him as she sprayed the air to get a whiff. Simon was having a ball rummaging through his private stash of occult substances. "I can't wait to come over so we can practice some magic," Simon shrieked excitedly as he clapped his hands and jumped up and down. See, Simon is more than just a magic shop dealer, he is a friend and accomplice to us sisters. Simon often comes over to the palace to play with us girls.

We gathered a bunch of stuff from the shop and bid Simon farewell. "Love you Sir Simon. See you soon," we told him as we hugged him goodbye. "Love you too," Simon replied as he pop kissed each one of us on our way out. Simon waved as we walked down the pebble pathway listening to wind chimes' song slowly fade.

CHAPTER 4

THE QUESTION

Ever since we were little, we would plan Sneak Out Parties. This was just a fancy term we made up for staying up late and practicing magic without mom and dad knowing. We used to wrap ourselves in bed sheets and pretend we were invisible as we tiptoed downstairs past the master bedroom. Now, we just joke about having Sneak Out Parties since we are all old enough to realize that bedsheets obviously don't hide you and our parents were never that oblivious to the fact that their daughters were sneaking downstairs to eat candy and stay up late. But we have fun calling our late-night meetings "SOP's" just for old-time's sake.

It seemed like it had been forever since all four of us had been living in the family palace at the same time. And at this point in time, all of us were close enough in age to really understand one another and actually want to hang out with each other. For the first time in who knows how long, we could actually practice our magic together as somewhat functional adult witches.

The thing was, we needed a purpose to practice magic. We have learned that practicing magic too frequently with no real intention, could be dangerous.

When the four of us arrived home from Simon's magic shop, we unloaded all our goods onto the kitchen table and examined our new supplies.

"Simon had some good stuff this time," Topaz winked.

Bayou misted her lemongrass spray in the air.

I picked up one of the potion bottles and admired the sparkling contents. "This might be just what we need to help us find The Answer to *The Question*..."

For a while now, we had been pondering The Question, and seeking The Answer. This question was no ordinary question. This was the greatest question of all time. This was the mother, the father, the sister and the brother of all questions. This was the biggest, most baffling, most perplexing, enigmatic question, unmatched by any other question out there. This was THE Question of all questions. Nobody had ever found The Answer before. Many had tried but none had succeeded. However, we were determined to figure it out. Maybe, just maybe, with a little help of magic, a touch of luck, and a brush with the divine, we could go on a quest and find what nobody had ever found out before. Together, maybe we could succeed.

"Do you really think we can do it?" inquired Bayou.

"I think mom and dad are going out tonight. Sneak Out Party later?!" Kaj asked excitedly.

CHAPTER 5

THE LUNAR EXPRESS

"Girls! We're going to a concert with Richie. We'll be back later!" Mom called from downstairs.

The four of us walked downstairs to say goodbye.

"What time will you be home?" Kaj asked Mom.

"Probably late. What are you girls getting up to tonight?"

"I think we are going to bake some vegan cookies and watch a movie," replied Topaz.

"Aww how cute! That sounds fun. Well, I don't think the concert ends until midnight and then we might go to Cigar Bar so we probably won't be home 'til late. Are you sure none of you girls want to come with us?"

Mom and Dad were always partying. Somehow it kept them young.

"No, we're fine. We kinda just wanna stay in tonight," said Bayou.

"Okay. Well, have fun and see you later!" Mom moved in

closer to give us each a hug.

"You too! Have fun! Love you," I responded.

One by one, we hugged Mom and Dad saying "I love you" and "goodbye."

As soon as the door closed behind them, we looked at each other and started dancing.

"Woo!!! Party time!!" exclaimed Kaj as she twerked.

Topaz was doing some weird Egyptian-looking dance move while I whirled around with my bird on my shoulder and Bayou frolicked about singing a made-up song.

This was the perfect opportunity for us to take our witch-craft skills to the next level.

We locked the front door, turned off the lights, and walked upstairs to Kaj's room. Kaj plugged in her fairy lights and cleared some of the mess from the floor so we could sit down.

"Are you guys ready?!" I asked.

The four of us looked at each other, unsure but with a mischievous passion in each of our eyes.

We prepared by gathering our supplies. We all sat in a circle on the wooden floor next to Kaj's bed. We put all of our sorcerous substances in the middle. Topaz distributed the tonics, formulas, herbs and potions evenly amongst the four of us.

"Maybe we should set our intention," spoke Bayou. "That's what I do in my yoga classes."

We all agreed that was a good idea.

The four of us held hands and silently set our intention. Because we were seeking The Answer to The Question, we would need all the help we could get.

"Okay," started Topaz, "first, you will need to eat this," she said as she held something up. "Then, light this on fire," she continued, holding something else up. "After, sniff this," she said, holding up a third substance. "And finally, put a single drop of this on your palm and place your hands above your heart as you close your eyes and imagine the unimaginable." She also said some stuff about how all of the various substances worked together to inhibit this or stimulate that, but none of us fully understood what she was talking about.

As we held our supplies in our hands, ready to follow Topaz's instructions, we prepared ourselves.

"Ready guys?" I asked.

My sisters nodded in agreement. We did exactly as Topaz advised, and then we recited the spell…

> *"As we seek the Answer to The Question,*
> *We're not quite sure what we hope to find.*
> *We intend to go on a journey,*
> *That in turn will blow our mind.*
>
> *While many have pondered The Question,*
> *The Answer has yet to be answered before.*
> *We know the quest will be quite the challenge,*
> *But answers come to you when you explore.*
>
> *So, show us what you will show us,*
> *And let us uncover what you wish to expose.*
> *We want to learn the secrets,*
> *That no other seemingly knows."*

And just like that, the magic was on.

We opened our eyes and looked at one another.

"What just happened?" Bayou asked.

"Do you guys feel anything?" inquired Kaj.

"I don't know," I said.

Topaz just looked around without saying a word.

"Oh well. Want to go downstairs to brew some tea and make some cookies?" asked Kaj. "Maybe we can try another spell later."

We followed one another down the stairs. I turned on a light in the kitchen while Topaz grabbed a pot to boil water for tea and Kaj turned on some music.

Bayou opened the sliding glass door to the patio and called us over to look at the glowing full moon.

We stood in awe at the majestic, celestial body, when all of a sudden, something else caught our eye. Something other than the moon lit up the night sky. We all looked at one another, dumbfounded.

The flying machine moved closer and closer until we were able to get a better look at it.

"Does that say 'The Lunar Express'?" I asked, squinting my eyes to get a better look.

"Sure does," smiled Topaz.

"Maybe they are here to tell us The Answer!!" shrieked Kaj.

The vessel got louder, brighter, and more powerful as it moved in close enough to create a strong whirlwind. The draft gusted all of our hair in a tangle and the blazing lights had all of us blinking our eyes in shock.

Then, all of a sudden, we were taken for a ride.

All aboard The Lunar Express.

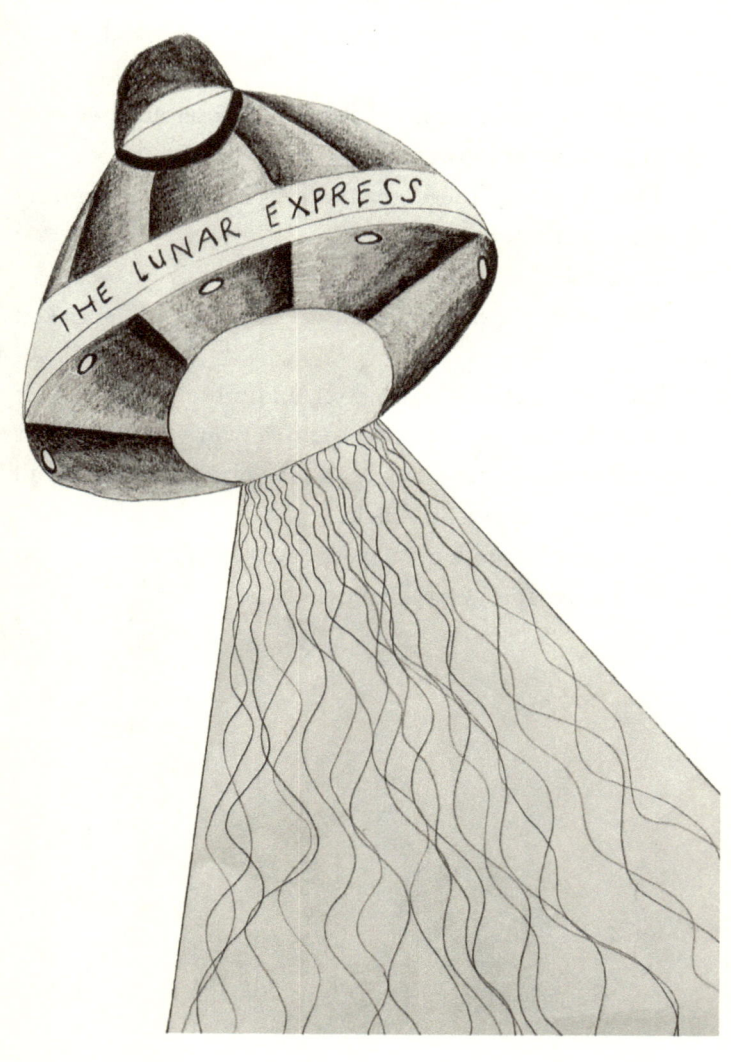

ANOTHER HERE

CHAPTER 6

GOLD TOWN

Eternity in a moment. That is the only way to describe the trip aboard The Lunar Express. The ride was over before it began. We arrived at our destination, shaken up, discombobulated, wonderstruck and confused as hell.

"Where are we?" shrieked Bayou.

"What just happened?" I inquired.

"Did we die?" mumbled Topaz.

"Is this a dream?" asked Kaj.

As we stood up and looked around, we tried to make sense of the darkness around us.

Rubbing our eyes, we spotted some lights off in the distance.

"Maybe we should make our way over to wherever that is," I said as I pointed to the faint glow in the distance.

Without any other real options, we headed toward the unknown flickering of lights.

As we moved in closer to the sea of lights, we felt a peculiar sense of lost familiarity toward this place.

"I feel as if I've been here before," exclaimed Bayou.

We all agreed this place seemed like somewhere we had seen before, maybe in our dreams or another life.

As we entered the city gates we saw a sign that said "Gold Town."

We immediately realized how the city got its name as all of the buildings sparkled with golden light.

"Wow, this place is beautiful!" said Kaj.

We stood in awe at the glistening city blinded by the twinkling golden gleam. We were taken aback when a man approached us.

"What are you girls doing here?" asked the strange man.

He was tall and wrinkled and wore a top hat embroidered with different crystals and stones.

"Umm, we don't know..." said Topaz.

The strange man smirked and commented on how us girls looked a little lost.

"Well that's for sure," said Kaj.

"We are actually really confused as to how we ended up here," I told him.

"We were abducted by the Lunar Express," said Bayou.

The stranger looked at us curiously as he scratched at his goatee. "I see..." he started. "Do you girls have any idea where you are?"

I told him that we saw a sign that said "Gold Town," hoping this stranger could offer some sort of guidance.

The stranger laughed and said "well, yes, this little town is called Gold Town. But you girls are not just in another town. You are in another *place*. You are in Another Here."

None of us could comprehend what he was saying.

"The Lunar Express doesn't just pick up anyone and bring them here," he continued. "You girls must have been up to something in order to be brought here."

The four of us were perplexed. It took us a minute to figure out what was going on before it hit us.

"The spell! It must have worked!" shouted Topaz excitedly.

"We were seeking The Answer to The Question. Would you happen to know anything about The Answer?!" asked Kaj.

The stranger started laughing hysterically. "Hahaha! You girls have been pondering The Question now have you? Well, I will tell you this much, nobody is gonna give you The Answer to The Question here. But I won't stop you from seeking. Who knows, maybe you will find answers to questions you didn't even know you had," he winked. "On another note, you have traveled a great divide to get to this very place in time. It wouldn't be fair for you to leave without fully experiencing Another Here. It's not every day you get to enter another dimension. Why don't you girls let me take you for a drink?"

We all looked at one another, a little skeptical about where we were, who this man was, and what we were doing. But we all just sort of shrugged and followed the man deeper into wherever we were.

As we walked down the streets of Gold Town, things got more and more interesting. Gold Town was booming with funky music playing throughout the streets, characters dressed almost as if it was some sort of Halloween bash, and bustling bars and clubs where every single Gold Town resident seemed to be hanging out.

The stranger finally introduced himself as Mandrake. After a quick tour of a few of Gold Town's busiest streets, Mandrake stopped in front of a little place that one wouldn't necessarily find on one's own. The front door was covered in vines and there was no sign out front.

"Welcome, ladies. This is my favorite spot in all of Gold Town."

Mandrake motioned for us to follow him inside.

The five of us found a small table tucked away in the back, left corner. The place was busier than we could have expected. There were small tables surrounded by couches and little wooden chairs. The place was dimly lit by the faint flicker of candlelight. Everyone seemed to be engrossed in their own conversations, chatting quietly over drinks. There were a few people sitting alone, reading, smoking, or just observing. After we sat down, a woman came over and gave Mandrake a kiss on the cheek. "The usual?" she asked. Mandrake nodded and held up his five fingers letting her know he wanted five of whatever his usual was. "That's Lilliana. She's a doll," Mandrake told us.

"This place is so cool," I said, admiring the strangely homey atmosphere.

"Yea, it feels like we're back in time!" said Kaj.

"Time..." Mandrake repeated slowly, smirking.

We all looked at one another, halfway wondering who this crazy man was, where we were, and what was going on. But our contemplative thoughts were interrupted when Lilliana brought over our drinks and set them on the table.

"Thank you, my dear," Mandrake whispered to Lilliana.

She smiled and walked away.

Mandrake picked up his glass and exclaimed, "Cheers children!"

"What is it?" Bayou asked.

"Nothing you've ever heard of," replied Mandrake.

All four of us looked at each other once again trying to read in each other's eyes what to do.

Kaj picked up her glass with a smile and clicked her glass to Mandrake's without further thought.

We all just laughed and followed along to cheer our new friend, trusting in it all.

"Wow, it tastes really good," said Bayou. "I've never tried anything like it."

"Tastes like heaven," said Topaz.

Mandrake smiled and said, "just wait and see how it makes you *feel*."

Mandrake went on talking away about the city of Gold Town and everything there was to do and see there. Sometimes he would speak random sentences that didn't really flow with whatever he was talking about. But we all just laughed and listened and laughed some more.

"Gold Town is an ancient place. It glows with the efficacy of the sun and vibrates with the power of the moon. But one can easily get lost here. Beings from all over come here and lose themselves searching. I know because I came here and never left. We're all searching for something that's already found us. But hell, I guess it's all the same everywhere. The perpetual process of searching, finding, and forgetting. And, well, Gold Town is a dazzling place, so here we are."

We all nodded in agreement.

"I was wondering, what does your name mean?" I asked Mandrake. I've always wondered if names somehow have deeper meanings.

"Well, Mandrake is actually a root found on planet Earth. It is a very special root. The mandrake root is used for so many things. Many witches, like yourselves, use it in magic rituals… In small doses, it can be used to treat things such as melancholy and mania, but when taken in large amounts, it rouses madnessss!"

Mandrake looked a little crazy as he spoke about his name. We silently agreed his name suited him perfectly.

When we all finished our drinks, Mandrake asked us how we were feeling.

"Really good!" exclaimed Bayou. "Everything has a magical shimmer to it."

"Everything looks more alive. *I feel* more alive," I said.

"Great!" shrieked Mandrake. "Now, let's move along."

We followed Mandrake out and back onto the streets of Gold Town. We walked in and around alleyways connecting larger roads charged with otherworldly characters. Everything was chaotic yet orderly. Everything flowed- the streets, the people, the buildings, all of Gold Town flowed in an enchanting way.

"Where are we going?!" Kaj asked Mandrake.

"You just wait hunny buns. We'll be there soon."

Eventually we arrived at a big building. There were lots of people outside, dressed eccentrically, making their way into the building.

"Well, this is where we say goodbye," shouted Mandrake over the crowds of people.

Then, just like that, he quickly walked away. We indistinctly heard him shout something from off in the distance. It sounded something like, "have fun in space!"

CHAPTER 7

SPACE

"What the…" started Kaj.

"Well, that was weird," exclaimed Topaz. "Where did he just go?"

We all started laughing a little nervously, wondering what was going on.

Then, all of a sudden, a man approached us. He had a similar look to Mandrake except he was much younger. He had long brown hair that had a golden light to it. The top hat on his head was embroidered with some interesting design and he wore a pair of spectacles containing Metatron's cube in one of the lenses.

"Hello siSTARS! Mandrake told me to take you to Space."

"You know Mandrake?" asked Bayou.

"Sure do. He's my brother."

We were all a little confused since Mandrake was WAY older than this man.

"Really? He seems much older than you…" I said.

"Hahaha, well, you know what I mean," winked Mandrake's "brother."

We weren't exactly sure what he meant but we smiled.

"Follow me."

Without much thought, we followed this new strange man into… Spaaaccceee.

Space was a jungle of sounds. It was a playground for people to dance and get lost and found in themselves amongst each other.

We realized we never caught the name of our new friend. But Space was loud and we couldn't really make out what he said. It sounded something like King-ill, so that's what we called him.

King-ill seemed to know everyone in Space. He had his own private space in Space, where some of his friends met up with us. King-ill took us up and down and all around the different areas of Space. It was all so dreamlike. Every room was booming with noise and moving with flashing lights. I guess you could call it a nightclub. Yea, it was a nightclub.

We followed King-ill to the dance floor, where we got lost in the music. Eventually, we decided to walk over to our home base area where some more of King-ill's friends had arrived. Then all of a sudden, I realized my reality had shifted. I was seeing things differently. I could feel an intense energy. I looked over at my sisters as we started to understand that the beverage we consumed with Mandrake was not your typical happy hour cocktail. Whatever we drank was potent and we were feeling all kinds of funky now. But in a good way!

Everything was moving and breathing. The entire place was alive. We felt alive.

I sat down next to Kaj for a moment while Bayou and Topaz went off to dance some more. Then, as more people started to arrive, one of King-ill's friends came over and started dripping some sort of liquid into people's mouths. He was wondering if Kaj and I wanted some.

"What is it?" I asked.

He said, "for all intents and purposes, let's just call it Gold's Hypnotic Bliss, or just G for short."

I had never heard of the stuff but I was enjoying the moment and I thought, "what the heck?" as I opened my mouth.

Kaj said she had heard of the substance because Simon sold it at his sorcery shop! She said Simon had informed her of how magical it could be, but that it could also be deadly.

"Deadly?!" I started to worry a little, though I knew there was nothing I could do now.

"Yea, but only if you take too much. It's like anything!" Kaj said, trying to calm me down.

I told Kaj that maybe she shouldn't take any, just in case.

"Don't worry, Aella. I want to."

Kaj opened her mouth despite my concern. As her older sister, I felt obligated to protect her, but I also knew she was an individual and was free to make her own decisions.

Bayou and Topaz had been off dancing but when they returned, Kaj and I told them we had just been given Gold's Hypnotic Bliss.

"What's that?" asked Bayou.

"Not exactly sure," I told her.

"Let's party!" Topaz said as we all started to shimmy and shake. We followed one another to a small stage that overlooked the crowded dance floor. One by one, we climbed up on to the stage to dance. Now, I don't know if it was Mandrake's drink, Gold's Hypnotic Bliss, the music, or Space itself, but we were feeling more powerful than ever. We were all tapped into not only the energy around us, but also the divine energy within ourselves.

"We are goddesses!" I shouted to Kaj as I looked down upon all the male energies mesmerized by the four of us dancing above them.

"Let her out!" Kaj called out, referring to the divine goddess within.

"I am so in touch with my Svadhishthana chakra right now," said Bayou.

Topaz smiled seductively and continued to dance.

We danced on stage for what felt like forever. We were so in touch with our divine feminine energies. I saw some other females out on the floor below us watching us dance, and I encouraged them to get up and dance with us, recognizing the goddess in each and every female energy.

Eventually, we got tired of being on display so we met King-ill on the dance floor, to be amongst the crowds. Out on the dance floor, different male energies came to dance with us. Some we chose to dance with, while others irked us.

"I'm getting a creepy vibe from some of these guys!" said Kaj as she made a face. I laughed at the funny expression Kaj made, but then realized she was kinda right. Some guys would just come over and try to put their hands all over us without even knowing us. We had to fend off a few disturbing ones before meeting some guys we each connected with.

I felt as if King-ill was our protector for the night. He made sure to watch over us as we all danced. It was amazing to feel the energy of people as well as the energy between people. All the souls in Space were vibrating on various frequencies.

I found myself dancing with one of King-ill's friends. He was the same man who blessed us with Gold's Hypnotic Bliss. We kept getting drawn to one another. The strange thing was, before we had even said anything to one another, I saw something in him. There was a magnetism between us that I could feel.

There was so much energy in Space, flowing and moving and somehow bringing different souls together. Some were brought together only briefly, while others were introduced for the first time in what would become a strong eternal connection. Only time would tell.

I looked over and saw each of my sisters dancing with someone.

All four of us were lost in SPACE.

Everything felt perfect.

And this lasted for a while. I don't know how long we were dancing in Space, but I'd say it was all night long.

Yet as it happens, every moment changes and eventually, it was time for us to move along. I didn't really want to leave. I didn't want all of this to end. But somehow, I knew it was time.

We realized we were very far from home, in some unknown crazy world, nowhere near finding The Answer to The Question, the only reason we were here in the first place.

Torn between leaving this moment, or moving on, we knew that change was inevitable.

Bayou and I expressed that we could easily spend more time here, not wanting to say goodbye.

Though the boys we met were cute and we wanted to hang out longer at the club, we knew that if we were meant to connect with these people again, we would.

"Nothing lasts, but nothing is lost," Topaz reminded us, quoting Terence McKenna.

She was right. Even though this moment couldn't last, we would hold the experience within us forever.

King-ill walked us out back onto the streets of Gold Town. We were almost blinded by the sun. It was light outside! We had arrived in darkness, but the sun had risen. We couldn't believe it!

"It's light out!" Topaz exclaimed.

We were shocked that so much time had passed since we'd arrived.

King-ill replied, "Time flies when you're in Spaaaaccceee."

Ain't that the truth.

We still weren't quite sure where we were or what was going on. But we knew we needed to get home soon or else mom and dad would flip out.

"Thank you for everything," I said to King-ill. "But now we just need to figure out how to get back home."

"Home?" asked King-ill.

"Yea, we're not from here," said Bayou.

"Where's here?" asked King-ill.

"Umm. I think Mandrake called it 'Another Here' or something like that," said Kaj.

"It's all here," replied King-ill. "But yes, I get what you mean. Well, if I were you girls, I'd try to hop a ride on the Electric Bug. He'll know just where to take you."

"What?" asked Topaz.

"Just go to the intersection of Street 11 and Avenue 11. You can't miss it. Goodbye for now goddesses!"

King-ill waved us off and disappeared back into Space.

EARTH

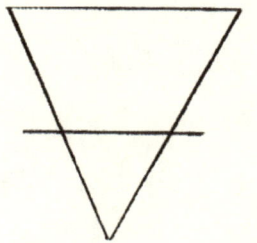

CHAPTER 8

THE UNDERGROUND

We made our way navigating through the streets of Gold Town. It was light out now but there was still a party happening in the streets.

"This place never sleeps," said Bayou.

Eventually we reached the intersection of Street 11 and Avenue 11, and King-ill was right. There was no way we could miss the Electric Bug. There was a giant machine-like ant sitting right on the corner of the road.

"This dream just keeps getting stranger and stranger," said Topaz.

We walked over to the big ant to check him out. To be honest, we were a little weirded out by him.

All of a sudden, the ant started communicating with us. He sure wasn't speaking any human language, but somehow, we understood him.

We told the ant that we needed to get home and we were

directed here by a friend.

"Well," spoke Mr. Ant, "you've come to the right place. Hop on in and I'll take you where you need to go."

If we were confused by any of the other strange stuff that had already happened to us, we were even more baffled now. Did this giant mechanical ant actually want to give us a ride? How?

Anyways, just as we were thinking all kinds of confused thoughts, a door on the side of Mr. Ant opened. We looked at each other, shrugged, and followed one another inside.

The insides of Mr. Ant were clean and orderly. He was like a big, sleek car. Kind of like a limousine, except much, much nicer.

We weren't sure how Mr. Ant was going to get us home, but we trusted him, sort of.

As we buckled in, Mr. Ant asked if we wanted to listen to some music.

"Sure!" we replied in unison.

Something about all of this was exciting!

We started dancing and singing to the tunes Mr. Ant turned on, temporarily forgetting we were inside a mechanical ant that was supposedly taking us home.

We could feel that we were moving but we were so caught up with listening to the music, we didn't realize how fast we were going. Mid-dance move, we were shaken up by a hard stop.

As we were all shoved forward, we looked at each other wondering if what just happened was normal. I mean, we had never actually taken a ride inside an ant before so what did we know? Yet, for some reason, we could sense something was up.

There was silence for a few moments before Mr. Ant spoke to us.

"Umm... ladies... umm... well, I think you girls should get out here."

"What?" I asked. "Where are we?"

"Well, we are currently in the Underground," continued Mr. Ant. "It's a beautiful place, really. You girls will make it home soon enough. It's just that we've...umm... run into some technical difficulties..."

None of us understood what was going on but I started getting worried. What if we never made it home? Mom and dad would be devastated. They would have no idea what happened to us. We should have never tried out that spell. I knew it was a mistake. Who was I to think that we were ready to take on something as big as The Question!? What were we thinking??

Frustrated, annoyed, and nervous, we all stepped out of Mr. Ant.

Upon leaving Mr. Ant, we realized we were in some strange underground world. It was almost as if we were in some big tunnel.

"What do we do now?" I asked Mr. Ant, looking around and not seeing any sign of where to go next.

"Oh, don't worry. You girls will figure it out."

Was he serious? Was he really going to just leave us here like this?

Just like that, like a train that had just dropped us off at our next stop, he continued on through the tunnel, leaving us all on our own.

"Well, what now?" asked Topaz.

We all looked at each other, at a loss of what to do, when I noticed a moth flutter by. It landed on the wall of the Underground. Something about it mesmerized me. As it flew by, I caught glimpses of its golden tint. I walked over to the wall where it landed to study it a little bit more. My sisters all followed behind. The four of us surrounded the moth, studying the intricate patterns on its wings, entranced by its golden glow. I realized that I never pay much attention to these insects that are quite beautiful. As we all stared at it, something was communicated to us. "Walk onward," we heard, though we didn't know exactly where the message came from.

We all looked at each other and took it as a sign. Without further thought, we started walking. Where we were going, we didn't know. As we walked through the Underground, everything felt very cave-like. Small passageways would lead to irregular large rooms with little tunnels taking us further along the Underground. We entered a big open space and noticed a bunch of bats flying around the ceiling. "Whoa!" said Bayou. "Look at that!" she said as she pointed up. It was unreal. So many bats! The bats were communicating in such a high-pitched sonar, it took us a few minutes to notice the music playing from a nearby room.

"Do you hear that?" asked Bayou.

We all took a couple of minutes to adjust our ears, but there was no doubt that music was playing.

"I think that's David Bowie," said Kaj.

We followed the sound. We walked through a tight tunnel that led to a random, medium sized room. As we got closer to the room, we could see a flickering of lights. Upon entering the room, we saw a bunch of lit candles lining the floor of the room. There was an incense stick burning, and "Blackstar" by David Bowie was blaring, echoing from wall to wall. But that's not all we saw. Sitting in the center of the room, with a purple, swirling, crystal ball, sat a young, beautiful girl. Her long, thick hair fell down on her lap and she had a deck of mysterious cards scattered about in front of her. Her eyes were closed but as soon as all four of us were gathered around her in the room, mouths wide open in shock, she opened her eyes slowly and smiled. "I've been expecting you," was all she said.

CHAPTER 9

ALL-SEEING-ALY

She obviously knew we were confused as to who she was and why she would be expecting us, so she gave us a brief introduction. "My name is Aly. Better known as All-Seeing-Aly," she winked. "I've been watching your girls' journey and I'm quite intrigued by all that you've been up to."

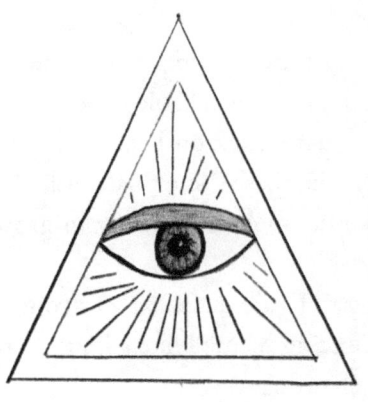

"Do we know you?" asked Kaj.

Aly laughed and said, "well, let's just say we met before, a long time ago. But I wouldn't expect you to remember it. Memory is a funny thing."

We all just stood there in silence before Aly continued, "Sit down, make yourselves comfortable. Would you like some tea?"

We all agreed a cup of tea sounded nice. Aly pulled out a chest filled with all kinds of various leaves and teas. "Take your pick."

None of us knew what any of it was, since none of it looked familiar and there were no labels or anything on any of the packs of leaves, so we all chose different random ones.

"Oooh, good picks!" said Aly as she started to boil hot water in a pot, over a small open fire pit.

As the water heated up, Aly went over to a little wooden cabinet to grab some mugs. Each mug was different from the next. All of the handmade mugs were dripping with colors and patterns, splattered with multidimensional paint. As she handed one to each of us, Kaj blurted out, "why do these mugs look so familiar?"

"I was hoping these would jog your memory," spoke All-Seeing-Aly, with an unmistakable grin on her face.

Kaj had a pensive look on her face, trying to figure this all out. "Did I make these?" she finally asked.

"You sure did," spoke Aly, her grin growing wider and wider.

I was trying to figure out what was going on. Everything we were experiencing seemed like a long, strange dream. But it was all so enchanting as well.

Aly decided to fill us in a little bit more, because let's face it, there was no way we were going to figure out what was up on our own.

As we sipped our tea, Aly spoke.

"Like I said before, I have been watching your girls' journey. I think you all know that you are currently in Another Here. Whether you realize it or not, you have chosen to come here. You are here for a reason. Though your seeking of The Answer to The Question has brought you here, that is not actually why you are here... You may not remember me, but we all know each other, from another place and another time. Kaj, you and I were, or should I say, are, best friends. I have been waiting to be reunited with you. I am here to help you unleash your powers, powers that are much needed right about now, for the good of ALL."

I looked over at Kaj and saw her tearing up. Kaj stood up and walked over to Aly, embracing her in a hug. I saw tears coming from the eyes of these two long lost best friends. There was soul recognition amongst all of us. It was beautiful. None of this seemed like a coincidence to me.

After a long embrace, Kaj sat back down and asked, "Okay, so what is it that we are here for?"

"Well, let me tell you a little bit more about what is going on here in the Underground," started Aly. "The Underground has been having some problems for quite some time now. There is a dark entity that has gained too much power and it is affecting everything. This entity is highly intelligent and contains a great amount of energy. Let me show you."

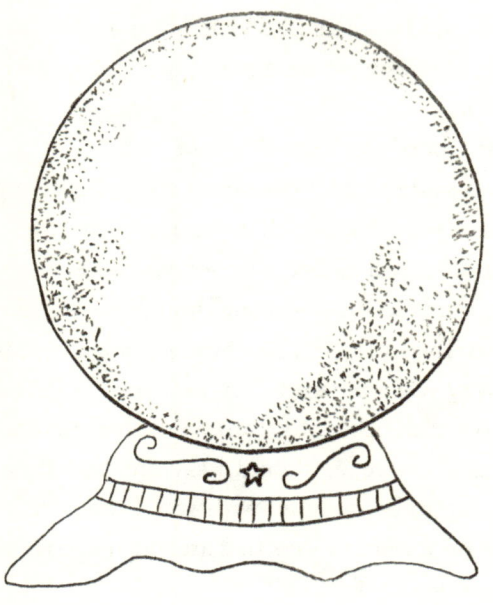

Aly closed her eyes and placed her hands over the purple crystal ball that sat in front of her. As she moved her hands around it, she started to hum a tune that sounded familiar. Then all of a sudden, we saw the insides of the crystal ball swirling with colors and images. When the swirling images started to settle, I could tell that what was currently being shown to us was the Underground. However, it wasn't the same Underground that we knew today. It looked like we were being shown the Underground as it was at a different point in time. The crystal ball revealed a place that was bustling with life. There were so many creatures, some recognizable, others not, all interacting and living harmoniously amongst each other. It looked like a balanced ecosystem.

"Is that Mr. Ant?" asked Bayou, pointing at the crystal ball.

"That is not the same Mr. Ant you girls met, but it is one of his kind," said Aly.

In the crystal ball version of the Underground I could see bats fluttering around, more Mr. Ants stampeding in an organized line, some big furry bear-like animals, humans, and some alien looking creatures I had never seen before. It seemed like the Underground was flourishing with life.

Aly continued, "At one point, everything was balanced. Of course, things tipped this way or that way from time to time, but it all worked itself out. However, at some point, the Gejus started to become highly intelligent. As their minds started to expand, so did their power and their ability to control the world of the Underground."

"Gejus?" I asked.

"Yes," said Aly pointing at the alien-like creatures in the crystal ball.

Aly paused for a moment before speaking again. "Before I continue, I want to preface this with the fact that not all Gejus are bad. Actually, none are all bad, or all good either, for that matter. However, with time, groups of Gejus have formed entities that have negatively affected everything. And greed and power is preventing these entities from changing their ways. Yet, there are groups of other Gejus that are fighting against these negative entities. It's a constant battle."

We all listened, trying to understand exactly what was going on. I wondered what these entities were doing that was so bad.

It was almost as if Aly read my mind.

She started, "With time, Gejus have manipulated the world of the Underground in such a way that would seemingly benefit themselves. The ways the Gejus live now is much different than they lived hundreds, thousands, even millions of years ago. Striving for better ways of life is important. However, the problem arises when life, in all forms, isn't respected. There needs to be a balance of give and take. As soon as nature starts being taken advantage of, consequences occur. As technical advances have been made, the Gejus have created a system that favors quantity over quality. When quality becomes totally disregarded, life is lost."

Aly placed her hand over the crystal ball to show us what she was talking about. She showed us various scenes of problems happening in the Underground. We saw the seven deadly sins; pride, greed, lust, envy, gluttony, wrath, and sloth. These were all displayed in various ways through the lifestyles and habits of the Gejus. Close your eyes and picture a dark world, a place where everything you fear is manifested. Imagine a place where all hope seems to be lost. This is what we were shown. We saw poverty, destruction, exploitation, and manipulation. And we could see that the dark energy affected everyone and everything. Even those that seemingly had "more" were no better off than those with less.

We also noticed that there were many humans living in the Underground, however, they were not the dominant force. As Aly had shown us, the Gejus were the most "advanced" species controlling the environment around them. It seemed to us that the humans were subservient to the Gejus, along with many other creatures. We saw humans exploited by the Gejus in various ways, whether it be for food, research, material goods, or entertainment. It was difficult to watch.

"While I am showing you the darkness," started Aly, "know that there is always more than meets the eye. Equal to the darkness, there is the light."

We still weren't quite sure why we were brought here.

Aly took a look at our solemn faces and said, "this situation is sad, but it's not hopeless. Nothing is hopeless, as much as it may seem so. Like I said before, not ALL Gejus are responsible for the darkness. In fact, it is really just the current system that needs some adjustments." Aly closed her eyes and stroked her long hair with one of her hands. She looked as if she was deep in thought.

I started to wonder what all of this meant. It seemed like such a mess. How could we help? What were we doing here? My head started to hurt and I imagined home. I imagined the palace my sisters and I dwelled in. I pictured my room and my bed. I thought about my bird Soleil and how much she meant to me. I saw mom and dad, the best parents anyone could ask for. I wanted to be back home, carefree, safe, and at peace. Yet, somehow, I knew that I needed to be here. Nothing was easy, but I... *we*, were called here for a reason. Ugh, why does life have to be so hard?? "Just breathe," I told myself. A voice in my head said, "this is where you are. Breathe. Recognize where you are and accept the challenge placed in front of you. You would not be here if you were not capable."

"Okay," I said to Aly. "What can we do to help?"

"Oh dear," Aly started. "Now that is completely up to you. I am only here to present the situation to you. I am here to show you what is and the problems at hand. But I cannot tell you what to do. That is for you girls to decide."

What? After all that, Aly couldn't even offer us guidance on how to help the situation? How were we supposed to combat a foreign entity that we had no real concept of that was spreading darkness through an entire underground world?

"Now girls, I will have to be leaving. But please stay here and make yourselves at home. I will leave you with my cards, my crystal ball, and this box of herbs. Use whatever you wish. And if you need to speak with me, you can just give me a call."

Aly slowly made her way over and into a narrow passageway we hadn't even noticed.

CHAPTER 10

STEALING POWER

"Give her a call?" asked Kaj. "How?"

Topaz walked over to a corner of the room to sit by herself for a few minutes. She started to meditate.

We all decided to sit quietly for a few moments and just be. I started thinking about where I was and what was going on around me. I was here with my three sisters, in some strange world, where a number of characters seemed to enter our lives. We had gotten here by casting a spell. Maybe we needed to cast another spell to fix this whole mess. Aly had told us that we were here for a reason. Something told me that we had everything we needed to succeed.

The four of us slowly gathered around the deck of tarot cards Aly had left behind for us.

All of us girls had decks of tarot cards at home and we used them all the time, mostly just for fun. However, maybe Aly's cards could help us now. I picked them up and shuffled them. I let each of my sisters choose a card from the deck, laying them face down on the ground in the order they were chosen to signify past, present, and future or shadow, soul, and let two become one.

One by one, I flipped them over.

As soon as I flipped them over, I noticed movement in the cards. These weren't the typical tarot cards with an image and some words. These were like mini virtual realities within themselves.

"Now that's trippy," I said, as my sisters and I all stared at the three cards in awe.

The card for the past/shadow was titled "Play." It displayed four girls on it, playing in various ways through music, travel, books, movement, and art. At the bottom of the card it said, "Play is essential. Manifestation arises from wonder and bliss."

The card for the present/soul was titled "Power of One." The card had a circle on it, swirling with numbers. The numbers started at one and continued swirling inward, infinitely. At the bottom of the card were the words "It starts with YOU. You are the one."

The card for the future/let two become one was titled "Love." There was an image of a man and a woman, moving closer to one another, as night turned to day and flowers bloomed all around them. The bottom of the card read, "Your love is eternal."

My sisters and I stared at the cards in front of us, wondering what they meant. We sat there and tried to decipher them one by one, looking for some kind of direction with the situation at hand.

"Play... I wonder if this card represents us in the past, practicing magic in a playful way," said Bayou.

Magic had always been a part of our lives, but mostly we just used it for fun. We'd always just used magic as a way to get insight on our love lives or help us figure out what moves to make next in life. It was always just a fun, playful way of getting in touch with the divine. And being playful is essential to life. It's how you grow and evolve, without even realizing that's what you are doing.

"That one is me," said Kaj, pointing to one of the girls on the Play card. The one that Kaj was pointing to had music notes coming out of her mouth as she was singing and dancing while skipping barefoot through a forest.

We all laughed. Whenever four girls starred in a movie or appeared in a book or in a picture, we'd always choose which one was each of us. Honestly, it didn't even have to be four girls. We'd assign random animals in movies or other characters to each of us depending on their role and personality. It was just a fun thing to laugh about.

Topaz pointed to another girl on the card and said, "that's definitely me." It totally was. The girl on the card was sitting in the corner reading next to a burning candle. It also looked like she had paint splattered all over her face and body.

"And that one is me," said Bayou pointing to the girl that was doing some move that looked like a crazy yoga pose in some underwater world.

And I was obviously the last girl on the card, flying through the air, traveling somewhere, holding something in my hand that looked like a writing utensil.

"Whoa, that is definitely us," I said.

Ok, so in the past we were playing. We were having fun and ultimately learning from our experiences. So, what about the present?

We looked at the present card at hand. Power of One… what could that mean?

As we all stared at the present card at hand, I think it hit each one of us in a strangely personal way. "It starts with YOU. You are the one." Deep down, I knew I had the power to make major changes, as does each one of us. And I think my sisters all felt the same. With every single thing we do, we change the world in some way or another.

Kaj held the future card in her hand. Love. "Maybe this means we're going to meet our twin flames!" said Kaj.

We all sort of smiled and pondered the idea of meeting our other halves…

"Well, now what?" asked Topaz.

We all looked at each other and started laughing. Here we were trying to analyze these tarot cards, looking for a sign or an answer. Were we even making any progress? Did we just make all this up in our heads? Ultimately, any cards we would have chosen would lead us to some sort of contemplation. And maybe it was this contemplation that was important. Maybe by looking for a sign, whatever that sign may be, it would somehow lead us back to our thoughts, a way of figuring out what to do by looking within. All these outward signs take you in. And that's where the real answers are.

We all sat and thought for a few moments. After some discussion, we decided that maybe it was time for another spell.

Now it was just time to figure out what kind of spell to cast. As much as we like to play with magic, we are all still just amateurs. So, figuring out what to do wouldn't come without difficulty.

I saw a bunch of herbs on the floor and decided to walk over and look at them.

I picked up bag after bag and read the names aloud. "Drameinis Bloode, Silver Samana Dust, Helltoare, Vernictilis, Roa…" I had never heard of any of these. I picked up a few more which were more familiar: "Frankincense, Lion's Mane, Dill, Sage, Mandrake."

"Mandrake? Why does that sound familiar?" asked Bayou.

We all thought about it for a moment before we remembered our friend in Gold Town, the very first person we met in Another Here. Man, that felt like a lifetime ago. So much had happened since we first arrived. How long had we been here?! There was no way of knowing.

"All these herbs must be used for different things," said Topaz, grabbing more bags of herbs from the pile.

"Do you know what they are good for?" I asked.

"Not really," Topaz replied. "I haven't heard of most of them."

I started thinking to myself, wondering what to do. We had access to all these herbs but none of us knew what any of them were used for. How could we cast a spell without any knowledge on what to do?

I walked over to the crystal ball sitting on the floor in the center of the room. I wondered how it worked. I sat down next to it and put my hands over it. Right away I noticed a swirling motion happening on the inside.

All my sisters walked over, mesmerized by the colorful swirls dancing inside the ball.

"Wow, that's so cool," said Bayou.

"I wanna try!" said Kaj.

I lifted my hands and let Kaj give it a go. I watched her as she sat cross-legged next to the crystal ball, eyes closed, hands moving slowly over it. Quietly she started to speak. "Show me Sam." Just like that, an image of Sam, Kaj's earthworm, appeared inside the crystal ball. He/She was chillin' in the dirt, somewhere.

"How'd you do that??" asked Topaz, overly excited.

"I don't know. I just asked," said Kaj.

I started wondering what else the crystal ball could show us.

"Let me try again," I said.

I sat down beside the ball and put my hands over it. I didn't say anything aloud, but I thought in my head about Soleil, my beloved macaw. I wanted to see her. Sure enough, she appeared. She sat atop her perch outside our precious palace, grooming her blue and yellow feathers. She looked so beautiful. I missed her so much.

"Omg, you didn't even say anything," said Bayou.

"I know! I just thought in my head and it appeared."

"I wonder what else this magic ball can be used for," said Topaz.

I thought long and hard. Maybe we could use it like the Internet. It seemed to be pretty powerful. Maybe we could look up spells!

I told my sisters that we needed to find a spell to help us get out of this mess. They agreed that was a good idea, but needed more direction. What kind of spell did we want to cast? At whom or what did we want to cast a spell at?

"What if we put a hex on the Gejus?" asked Kaj.

"Yea," started Bayou. "Maybe we should curse the Gejus that are spreading this darkness."

Sounded like a decent idea to me…

Topaz was on it. As she glided her hand over the crystal ball, she asked to be shown hexes. So many different pages popped up, like the Internet, but better. We came across a number of spells for cursing someone.

"Oh, let's look at that," said Kaj, pointing to a page in the crystal ball that displayed curses using herbs and potions. "Maybe we have all the right herbs here."

We took a look at The Hexes and Curses Black Magic Shopping Menu displayed in the crystal ball. Indeed, we did have quite a few of the herbs required for hexes.

We came across a video of a witch using Vernictilis mixed with Helltoare and a sprinkle of Shenkcha Q to conduct some Black Magic.

"I saw Vernictilis and Helltoare over in the pile of herbs," I said. "But I don't remember seeing Shenkcha Q."

"Well, maybe we can use something else in place of it," said Kaj. "We only need a sprinkle of it anyways."

While Kaj and Bayou were rummaging through the herbs, Topaz was searching the Dark Web Crystal Ball.

"Look what I found," said Topaz, pointing to something called "ZAP BE DEAD."

Whoa, something about this looked dangerous. "How did you find this?" I asked.

"I don't know," said Topaz. "I just started going deeper and deeper into the crystal ball until I got here, though a bunch of warnings popped up before I could enter."

"Warnings?" asked Bayou.

"What kinds of warnings?" asked Kaj.

"I don't remember," said Topaz. "I just kept entering, curious what I'd find."

"Well, let's take a look," I said.

We clicked on the spell called "ZAP BE DEAD."

Dark swirls, red flashing lights, and what looked like smoke, moved around in the crystal ball, making it hard to read the words that formed one after another, showing us a spell that made the four of us a little uneasy. We each read the spell, silently to ourselves.

"ZAP BE DEAD
GONE FROM MY HEAD.

I FORBID YOU STAY
CONDEMNED FARAWAY.

FOR SO MANY YEARS
NO MORE TEARS.

I ZAP YOU OUT
TO AN UNKNOWN WHEREABOUT.

I FORCE YOU THERE
TO THE LAND OF NOWHERE.

WHEN ALL IS DONE
THERE'S NOWHERE TO RUN.

ZAP BE DEAD
GONE FROM MY HEAD."

We all kind of just sat there before we agreed that this spell seemed a bit too intense for us. What exactly did "ZAP BE DEAD" entail? We weren't trying to kill the Gejus. We really just wanted to stop the destruction currently taking place.

"What other options do we have?" I asked my sisters.

"I don't want to kill anyone," said Kaj. "But maybe if we can somehow steal the power away from these dark entities, we can stop them from continuing with these practices."

"What if we use Black Magic to cut the technology that is assisting the Gejus in indulging in these sinful ways?" asked Bayou.

"Yea, if the Gejus didn't have access to the technology they are accustomed to using, that would stop them from abusing their power," said Topaz.

We decided to look through the crystal ball for spells that could help us out. Unfortunately, we really couldn't find anything specific to what we needed. After searching for a while, we became frustrated and started thinking about what to do next.

"Maybe we should give Aly a call like she said," I spoke to my sisters. "I bet she'd be able to guide us."

"Yea, but how do you suppose we do that?" asked Topaz. "It's not like any of us brought our cell phones with us."

"If I knew we were going to be abducted, I would have grabbed my phone," said Bayou. "I think I left it sitting on the kitchen table. Who knows how many times Mom has tried to call us. She must be so worried."

"Wait," said Kaj, "maybe we can reach Aly through the crystal ball!"

That was definitely a good idea. Kaj placed her hands over the crystal ball and asked to reach All-Seeing-Aly. There was a ringing noise for a few moments before Aly appeared.

"Ahh it's like Facetime!" said Kaj, as we all screamed with excitement. Aly just laughed at us.

"Can you see all of us?" I asked.

"I sure can," Aly replied. "So, what's going on? How's the planning coming along?"

"We're not sure," I said. "That's why we called you. We were thinking about putting a hex on the Gejus. We came across one spell called ZAP BE DEAD, but it gave us the chills. Now we are thinking of using Black Magic to take away the technical means the Gejus are using to spread darkness. We really just want to steal their power, in one way or another. We just can't find any spells specific to our purpose. We were hoping you could give us some direction."

"I see," said Aly, looking a bit skeptical. "Now I don't know what kind of hex you plan on putting on the Gejus, but I need to warn you girls that using Black Magic is very dangerous. I'm sure you already know, but any curse you put on another, be prepared to have it come back to you threefold. I am not telling you not to do it. Just think long and hard before you do. Hexes are a powerful thing and with the wrong intentions, much can go wrong. My advice to you is to sit down with each other and really think about what it is that you are trying to accomplish. From there you can look at all of your options and figure out the best route to take. I told you girls already that you hold a great power, and that is a special thing. But be wary. Use your power wisely. Many people misuse their powers, and that is when things go wrong. Just because you can do something, doesn't mean you should. Just think about it. You know what to do. And if you need me, just holla at your girl. I'll be right here." Aly smiled as she disconnected from us.

Aly was right. We really needed to think long and hard about what it was that we were trying to accomplish.

What was our ultimate goal? Our ultimate goal was to stop the Gejus from spreading darkness.

And how could we go about this? There were definitely different ways of going about this. An obvious one, kill the Gejus that were doing these evil acts. But we knew that was wrong. I mean none of us girls even had it in us to squash an ant. So that option was out. Then there was the option of stealing their resources. We could steal their supplies, factories, money, technology, and any other means of continuing on with the madness. But something about that seemed wrong too. Would stealing from them really make them stop? I guess it would put a halt to it all, but would it put an end to it in the long run? The same idea goes for killing. Would killing them end these acts?

It seemed to me that something much deeper needed to occur. There needed to be a shift in consciousness. Light needed to be shed on the issue in order for changes to occur. By bringing awareness to what was going on, only then would things change. I had seen proof of this countless times on

Earth. It seemed that levels of consciousness were constantly rising to higher and higher levels, mostly because of awareness.

So, how could we bring awareness to what was going on with the Gejus? I've always been a strong believer in words. By communicating and speaking about a topic, others can slowly start to understand. I think everyone is born with a moral compass. Knowing what is right and wrong isn't something that is taught, it is something that is known. But so many get lost in culture and society that they forget there is something beyond all that.

"What if we say a little prayer for the Gejus to awaken to the next level of consciousness?" I suggested.

My sisters agreed it wouldn't hurt, though it didn't seem like enough. It wouldn't put an immediate end to anything and much more suffering would occur before any changes were made. But it was a start.

We gathered around in a circle and held hands. We thought long and hard about our intentions. We realized we needed our intentions to be directed in a positive manner. Our intentions needed to be pure. Rather than directing any sort of negativity at the Gejus, we would instead intend for a powerful shift to occur for the good of all.

"Oh wait," said Topaz, right before we began, grabbing a candle to light and some sage to burn. "Aly left us with these herbs for a reason, right? Might as well use one we know."

Bayou directed us with our breaths and Kaj hummed a tune. We all sat, preparing for a spell to put our intentions out into the Universe, sending out seeds with our thoughts, hoping those seeds would penetrate through and grow.

We started:

"Being shown the madness around us,
We wish to bring light to the dark.
While many may not want to change things,
It begins with ONE to make a mark.

When we see an injustice occurring,
There is something that needs to be done.
For the evil that's imposed on another,
Is in turn inflicted back on everyone.

Let us raise our vibration together,
And learn from what's been done in the past.
Recognize the endless beauty that surrounds us,
And see that heaven is here at last."

There was more to be done, but this was the first step.
Shedding light on the dark is the ultimate way to steal power.

CHAPTER 11

THE GIFTED GEJU

At a loss of what else to do, we decided to go explore. Maybe something else would come to us along the way. Like Aly said, we should put some thought into whatever it was we were going to do.

We followed a cool, dark, narrow pathway that led us into a bigger room. From each room we entered, we'd find more little cracks and crevices that we could squeeze between to lead us further along. Soon enough, we reached a wide opening. The ceiling must have been way up high because we couldn't make it out. And for as far as our eyes could see, there was just vast open space. And within this open space, so much was happening. This place looked like a futuristic world. There were a mix of creatures living and interacting side by side. Gejus were using advanced transportation and technology to move from place to place and communicate with one another, humans were out and about, working and hanging out, bats were fluttering around, and other creatures appeared randomly from time to time.

We kept walking. We must have blended in because we passed by countless beings and none of them seemed to notice us. They were all caught up in whatever they were doing. Many of the Gejus seemed distracted by some strange screens that they had attached to the tops of their arms. We walked down a street that had a bunch of little shops. Most of them were selling things I didn't recognize. I also noticed advertisements popping up as we walked down the street. The advertisements were 3-dimensional, interactive realities fused with the "real" world. One of the advertisements was for what looked like a futuristic fast food restaurant. The ad offered two hammys for the low price of 1566 plats.

"I guess plats is the currency they use here," I said.

"What's a hammy?" asked Bayou.

"Looks like some sort of burger or sandwich," said Topaz as she interacted with the advertisement, reaching out her hand to the virtual hammy.

"What do you suppose those hammys are made from?" asked Kaj.

None of us could be certain, but we remembered Aly showing us a scene from a factory where large numbers of creatures, humans included, were raised for food, indoors under strictly controlled conditions intended to maximize production.

In a world that seemed so connected through technology, it seemed that so many of the Gejus living in it, were so disconnected from each other and from everything else around them.

Walking through the streets of the Underground brought on a sense of heaviness. We kept walking, not quite sure where we were going, yet somehow, we were intrigued by this underground world, as dark and cold as it was. As we continued along, I caught a glimpse of light coming from a little shop that was overgrown with moss and greenery. It was the first place I had seen that stood out from the other concrete blocks. Tucked between a shop selling something called Kratosphonic Tech Gear and another one titled Real Triferian Contra, was a little place called Awaken. There were fairy lights surrounding it and there was something about the glow of the place that called me to it.

"Let's see what that place is," I said to my sisters.

I opened the door and slowly walked in. The place smelled of some strange sort of earthly flavors. There were numbers and patterns drifting through the air and there was faint music playing. Upon entering, a human greeted us with a welcoming smile. She asked if we were here to meet with Una.

"Umm, no," I said. "We were just passing by and I was curious about this place."

"Oh," well, you should meet Una. "She'll be happy to see you. Follow me."

Behind a curtain on the other side of the room, sat Una.

We all must have looked very surprised to see that Una was a Geju. This was our first real close interaction with a Geju.

The human and Una communicated to one another, though neither of them were actually speaking. They must have been using some form of telepathy. The strange thing was, we were able to understand.

Una started speaking to us with her mind. She told us that most humans and Gejus were not able to communicate. She was gifted in her ability to do so and she could tell we were too. She told us that through her mental connection to The Divine, all the information she could possibly need came through her. She was here to help shift consciousness. She was here to help awaken the spirit in all.

We asked her questions and she gave us answers, though no one actually spoke a word.

Una told us that the current Underground world was out of whack. As the Gejus gained intelligence, they also gained power and control over the rest of the environment. And while most Gejus weren't actually "bad," they were all living under the current system. And something had to change.

We asked her if it was dangerous for us to be walking around in the Underground.

"It depends on where you are," she conveyed to us. "As you can tell, in this area, humans and Gejus live side by side along with many other beings with no real problems. Most Gejus adore humans. However, there are other areas where humans aren't safe because groups of Gejus look to capture them for personal gain."

We waited for her to elaborate.

"Think about where you girls are from for example. On planet Earth, there are certain creatures that are in situations much like the humans are here. Because humans are the 'most advanced' species on Earth, they play the same role the Gejus play in the Underground. While tons of humans on Earth live peacefully amongst other creatures, there are also tons of creatures that are subject to living hells at the hands of humans. Whether humans are using these creatures for food, entertainment, research, or material goods, there is a lack of respect for the lives of these other beings."

We started to understand. Una told us that what was happening on Earth was sort of mirrored in the Underground. It was almost like a dark subconscious mind of the human race, where our deepest, darkest fears were manifested.

"Things are constantly changing and believe it or not, there are tons of Gejus that are fighting to change the system in one way or another," said Una. "When one way of life is no longer sustainable, changes need to be made, whether by force or will. Nature has a way of working everything out. But if we can just work with nature, rather than against it, life will be much easier in the long run."

I closed my eyes for a moment and thought about my dreams. My dreams are almost always dark. Kaj says my Scorpio moon is to blame. But maybe my dreams take me to a place like the Underground, a collective subconscious world where I am shown a deep, dark place that needs healing.

Una spoke to us through a smile that said, "We are fighting for life, but often times we don't realize that it is ALL life. By not revering the life that is, we put ourselves in a hypocrisy. We fear death so much, we lose touch with life. We have forgotten that everything is life, continuing on and on in all of its beautiful forms. Everything is everything. And by hurting another, we are only hurting ourselves. We have lost touch with the spirit world, living only for the material. When we live in fear, we live in hell. It's all in our heads. When we wake up and realize it's all divine, suddenly we are no longer afraid. We are in heaven."

Wow, that really hit us. Everything Una communicated to us made so much sense. This Underground world was a shadow world, an obscurity of the human, fear-based thinking. And we were currently lost in it.

"So, what are we to do?"

"Go back home and shed light with your knowledge. The world is changing, every single second. Through all this darkness, comes light. Keep evolving and doing what's right and the rest will follow. It starts with you. Realize everyone is at a different stage of their journey. Don't judge them for where they are. Instead, focus on yourself and see the good that comes from following your truth. As slow as the process may seem, consciousness is constantly rising to higher and higher levels."

"So, we have nothing to do here?"

"It's all here, my dears." Una smiled again and told us that it was time for us to leave the Underground. She said it was time for us to make our way home, though there was still more for us to accomplish on our journey back.

I didn't feel as if we had accomplished much of anything so far. But Una reassured me that we had. Our minds had already been expanded by these experiences and moments of enlightenment. And what more could we wish to accomplish than to awaken to the truth?

Una informed us that All-Seeing-Aly was waiting for us.

She told us to meet her in the forest, by Silver Pond next to the willow tree.

So, off we went in the direction Una pointed, deep into the Underground forest.

CHAPTER 12

SAM

It was really dark as we trekked through the woods. The trees were different from any I had ever seen before. And because we were in some underground world, there wasn't much light, especially amongst the twisted trees and vines that climbed up beyond our sight. As we stumbled over roots and pushed our way around hanging limbs, we started worrying that we were lost.

"Follow the fireflies," was the only advice Una gave us on how to find Silver Pond.

When we first entered the woods, there were tons of fireflies lighting the way for us. But now, there were fewer and fewer.

We stopped for a moment to catch our breaths and keep our eyes open to the glow of a firefly pointing us one way or another. But none of us could make out any lights. Kaj decided to sit down on a big root. She looked down at her feet and commented on how dirty they were. We all had dirty feet from trekking through the woods barefoot on the damp soiled ground. Then all of a sudden, we heard Kaj scream.

"What's wrong?" I asked her, worried.

Kaj picked something up out of the dirt with a surprised look on her face.

It took a moment for me to see what she was holding through the darkness. I could tell it was small but I wondered how something so tiny could have made her scream the way she did.

Then, all of a sudden, I saw it moving. I realized it was Sam, Kaj's beloved earthworm!

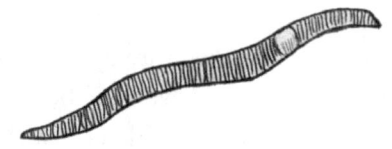

"What? How did you get here?!" I asked Sam.

"I just squirmed my way over," replied Sam.

"Maybe The Lunar Express abducted Sam too," said Topaz looking skeptical.

"I don't know what you all are talking about, but I sure am happy to see you! Kaj, I thought you were gonna step on me again!" Sam said, teasing Kaj about the day that they first met.

"I never stepped on you, Sam!" said Kaj rolling her eyes.

They always joked about stepping on one another.

Sam said if Kaj stepped on him/her, he/she would have to step on Kaj in return. "Ooooh! How scary! That would really hurt," she'd reply sarcastically to the puny earthworm.

We expressed to Sam that we were looking for Silver Pond and we were lost and contemplating what to do.

We were extremely surprised when Sam told us he/she loved Silver Pond and could tell us exactly how to get there.

"You've been here before?!" asked Kaj, speaking exactly what we were all questioning.

Sam looked confused by our question. He/She didn't know what we meant by "here." We tried to tell him/her about Another Here as this alternate dimension we were in but he/she had no idea what we were talking about.

"Maybe earthworms live in multiple dimensions?" questioned Topaz.

Anyways, Sam gave us perfect directions to Silver Pond, where we found All-Seeing-Aly sitting on the banks, looking like the angel that she is, holding her crystal ball between her legs, a bag of herbs in her left hand and something we couldn't quite make out in her right.

CHAPTER 13

LIGHT THE FIRE

As we got closer, we were surprised to find that what Aly was holding in her right hand was another living, breathing member of the family.

"Blaise?!" shouted Topaz, as she ran over to her fire-breathing lizard.

"What's with our spirit animals being here?" asked Kaj.

"Yea, how did they get here?" inquired Bayou.

"Oh, dimensions don't exist for spirit animals," said Aly. "Don't be surprised if your little turtle decides to pop up at some point, Bayou. And Aella, I'm sure your precious macaw, Soleil, will make an appearance when the time is right too."

"After everything we've seen, I don't think anything will surprise me anymore," I said.

"Oh, you'd be surprised," winked Aly.

Silver Pond glistened like a thousand stars were twinkling on the surface. I stood there mesmerized by the beauty of the glowing body of water surrounded by entangled trees and the sporadic fireflies lighting up our otherwise dark surroundings.

"Now girls," started Aly, "it is time for you to leave the Underground and start the next leg of your adventure on your way back home. Your work in Another Here isn't quite done yet. But you have served your purpose in the Underground."

"I don't feel like we've done much of anything," Bayou said.

"It never feels like you've done much of anything. But I assure you, you have," said Aly. "It's all in your head. You've started to understand much of the darkness that has taken place here in the Underground as well as on Earth. What you've experienced here, you will take home with you and you will continue to shed light on the darkness as you live your truth. Guide people with the words you speak and the way you do things. Lead by example. Know that it starts with you and ends with you."

"But we never stopped the Gejus from spreading darkness," exclaimed Kaj in a concerned tone.

"Like Una told you girls, the Underground is a mirror to the world you know back home. The way you can put an end to it, is to take action against the wrongs currently taking place back on Earth. Keep pushing to change the system for the better. Protect the natural world in any way you can. Mother Nature is living and minded, and the more you do to protect her and all of her creatures, the more she'll do to protect you. Respect all that she is. It may seem like a slow process, but you want to be on the side of progress. Those that think it's all hopeless, often fall into the category of those not willing to do anything to make the changes needed to be made."

"So, what now?" asked Bayou.

"Now it's time for a little spell…"

Aly gathered her things and motioned for us to come sit next to her by the pond.

She put the crystal ball in front of her, handed a bell to Bayou, a bag of herbs to Kaj, a golden pen and sheet of paper to me, and Blaise to Topaz.

Topaz pet her little iguana and gave him a big kiss. Like Topaz, Blaise is pretty quiet most of the time, unless he has something important to say.

"Are you girls ready? We are about to do some serious magic so I hope you girls are paying attention," spoke Aly. "Now before we start, I want to let you know that while I won't be joining you on this next leg of your journey, this isn't goodbye. I will be seeing you again, when the Universe wants it. But for now, I want to tell you that all you need, you have.

Trust the journey and know that wherever you are, is where you are supposed to be. Follow your intuition and the rest will fall into place. You may feel lost at times, but that's okay. You are on your way Home."

Kaj gave Aly a hug.

"Oh, one more thing," said Aly as she put her hands over her crystal ball.

The insides of the crystal ball started to swirl with colors and patterns before we could make out what we were being shown. It looked like there was some sort of shop inside the ball.

"Is that Simon's Sorcery Shop?" I asked.

Before Aly could reply, Simon popped up in the ball, shrieking excitedly at the image of the five of us staring back at him.

"AHHH! I am so happy to see you girls!!!" exclaimed Simon.

"Wait, do you guys know each other?" asked Kaj looking back and forth between Aly and Simon.

They both laughed.

"Well, let's just say we *all* know each other," said Simon with a smile on his face.

The strange thing was, it felt like we were all long lost friends or siblings or witches.

"How are you, Simon?" asked Bayou.

"I'm great! I can't wait to hear all about your adventure. Aly tells me it's been quite the journey. You'll have to come by my shop soon to visit me. I miss all of you so much!"

"What are you drinking?" asked Topaz as we watched him sip something green from a large clear glass.

"Oh, this is just some cactus juice I whipped up last night! I'll make some for you when you guys come home! Anyways, it's been great seeing you. Catch you on the flipside!"

Simon signed off and Aly told us that now it was spell time.

"Kaj, I need you to go through that bag of herbs and choose what we need," said Aly.

Kaj looked through the bag that Aly had handed her and started pulling out different plants, flowers, seeds and herbs.

"I don't recognize a lot of this stuff," said Kaj.

"Use your intuition," spoke Aly. "You are the element of earth. Let it speak to you."

Kaj used her senses to determine which herbs we needed for our spell. She grabbed some water from the pond and mixed some of the herbs with the glistening water, creating a tonic for us to drink. She set aside some dried fungus for us to eat. And other ones she mixed up and put into the little wooden pipe Aly brought with her for us to smoke.

Kaj looked at Aly before taking a sip of the tonic and then passing it around for each of us to drink. We then proceeded to eat the dried fungus. It tasted strange and earthy. Aly watched us all the while.

"Good," said Aly. Now I will start speaking the spell and when you hear your prompt, I need you to play your part. "Bayou, you will begin with the ringing of the bell and the rest will follow. Are you ready?"

We all nodded.

Aly started…

"Ring the bell
to start the spell.
Stop and listen 'cause
The Universe has something to tell.

Whatever you hear,
There's nothing to fear.
Things might not make sense,
But in time they'll be clear.

Now is the time to take note
Of all that you wrote.
It's all part of your story.
On and on you will float.

Hold these herbs in your hand,
And trust in the plan.
For you yourself are everything,
Push forward, expand."

Aly paused for a moment, looking for something.

"Oh no! I forgot a lighter," she said.

We all looked around trying to help her out when we heard a faint laughter coming from the direction of Topaz.

"What are you laughing at, Topaz?" I asked.

"I'm not laughing," she replied.

We realized it wasn't Topaz that was laughing. It was Blaise.

"What do you think I'm here for?" asked Blaise, smirking like a little green reptile.

Duh! Blaise could light us up no problem! While he may just be an iguana in the "real" world, he's a fire-breathing beast in this one.

"I knew you were here for a reason," Aly said to Blaise. "Okay, Blaise, I'm gonna need you to carefully light up these herbs so that the girls can get to where they are headed. Topaz, please assist your beloved dragon so that he doesn't blow anything up."

Blaise nodded his head up and down like iguanas do when they communicate with one another, and Topaz nodded her head in return.

Aly continued.

"Light the fire
to ignite your desire.
Off you go witches,
You're headed home, what awaits is an empire."

FIRE

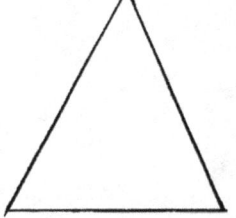

CHAPTER 14

THE LABYRINTH LIBRARY

We woke up in a large library. The four of us, and Blaise, were sprawled out across the wooden floor. We must have all opened our eyes around the same time, because we all had the same confused look on our faces as if we had just awoken from a crazy dream.

We got up to look around and figure out where we were. All we could see were shelves on both sides of us with books towering above us.

"Where are we?" asked Topaz, as she gently grabbed a book from the shelf and opened it.

We were all surprised when words immediately jumped out from the book, giving us some sort of answer to Topaz's question.

"Here you are. All is now."

Topaz closed the book and we all just stood there in awe. She put the book back in its place and we decided to walk along the towering shelves to see where they would take us. We realized the shelves formed a complicated network of passages.

As we followed the maze of manuscripts, we found ourselves being led down paths that didn't always lead to anywhere in particular. Every dead end left us confused and frustrated. We'd think we were getting somewhere, when all of a sudden, there'd be a wall blocking our path. We'd be forced to turn around and try another route.

After running into yet another dead end, we stopped and wondered what was going on.

"How will we ever get out of here?" asked Kaj.

"It seems every way we turn, our path gets blocked," said Bayou.

"Maybe we should grab another book and see what it says," I suggested.

Topaz ran her fingers along the spines of a few books. She took a couple of deep breaths and let her hands reach for whichever book she was drawn to. She slowly picked one off the shelf and opened it up. It spoke to us:

"Tap in. I am with you, always."

We looked around and all at once, our perception had shifted. We noticed a magical shimmer coming from the books around us as we realized we were being divinely guided.

Kaj grabbed another book and flipped to a page:

"Keep going."

We did just that.

Along the way, we encountered different works that caught each of our eyes. However, nothing had any labels or titles. It's like these books consisted of every thought, action, emotion, word, intent, and event from all time. Each book we picked up offered us some sort of guidance or clue as to where we were going. It seemed we were immersed in timeless wisdom. We had access to the minds of every soul that had ever existed from the past, present, and future.

The labyrinth took us deeper and deeper into this complex network of intelligence.

"It's a little chilly in here, don't you think?" asked Bayou, shivering, as we continued on through the maze.

We all agreed the library was a little bit cold. It was also a little bit dark.

Upon hearing us, we noticed Blaise jump onto the book-shelf and start climbing up.

"Blaise, where are you going?" asked Topaz.

Blaise didn't answer. He climbed up a few shelves and then let out a huge roar. We were all taken aback by not only the booming sound that came from the tiny green dragon, but also by what happened next. We watched a stream of fire fly out of Blaise's mouth and onto a torch. The torch must have been connected to a network of other torches lining the shelf, because one by one the torches lit up like dominoes, illumi-nating our path and creating some added warmth.

Blaise jumped down and proceeded to do the same thing on the other side. We could see the flickering of lights for as far as our eyes could see both in front of us and behind us, a trail of fire creating a warm glow above us. On Blaise's way down from the shelf to our left, he accidentally knocked over a book. It fell to the floor, opened up, and spoke to us:

"Welcome to the Labyrinth Library, sisters."

We were all taken aback by these words that came out from the book.

"How did the book know we would end up here?" asked Bayou.

Kaj picked the book up from off the floor and flipped the page. Out came the words:

"It is written."

Kaj flipped to another page and we noticed that it was blank, but not for long. Words slowly started to form out of nowhere:

"You are writing it as you go."

Kaj closed the book and put it back on the shelf.

"This is a strange story," said Topaz.

We continued to follow one another down the fire-lined walls of books. Topaz, the biggest book-lover I know, was mesmerized by all of the books surrounding us. It wasn't long before she felt the urge to stop and choose another book off the shelf. When she opened it up, out popped the words:

"You must have been up to something quite extraordinary to be here, now."

We thought about that for a moment. We weren't quite sure how we ended up here in the first place. We were seeking The Answer to The Question and then all of a sudden, we were abducted by The Lunar Express. We decided to ask the library for any insight into The Answer.

We closed our eyes and asked to find the answer.

Topaz grabbed another book and opened it up. Out popped words by Terence McKenna:

"The problem is not to find the answer, it's to face the answer."

Topaz was elated to receive these words of wisdom from Terence McKenna, someone that has been a great influence on the way she thinks.

I thought long and hard about what he said.

Facing it.

With Terence's words on facing the answer, I started to think about life and death. What is life? And what is death? The waltz between life and death is something so precious, so ephemeral, so unbelievably romantic. And in this life, facing death is something we all have to do, sooner or later.

As I pondered the cavort between life and death, I decided to grab a book and open it up. The book told me:

"Death is inevitable. But death is not the end. Death is a transformation. Death is life, in another form. Nothing ever really dies."

Interesting… I started to think more about this. It seems to me that life is constantly building to greater and greater complexity. Maybe with each death and rebirth, life becomes filled with more.

I looked at the library around me and I realized that every single book held keys to the past, present, and future through the accumulation of wisdom acquired through time. Topaz, the most well-read person I know, is seemingly always quoting people who have influenced her through their words. Though many of these writers may no longer be alive, somehow their thoughts live on, through Topaz, and through everyone else who accumulates bits and pieces of their wisdom. We are all connected. Everything from the past has built up to what we know now. I thought about Topaz and how she has been such a major influence on the way I think. So many of the books and ideas she introduced me to opened my world to the worlds of those who wrote them. And through these authors, philosophers, and poets, we gain access to those that influenced *them*.

Bayou grabbed a book and opened it up:

"It's this multiplication of ideas that are living in the present moment."

I thought about how we, as humans, hold so much knowledge and wisdom, though we can hardly grasp even a fraction of what is *actually* happening.

I started to wonder about the future and what it held for us humans. In just a short amount of time, humans have changed the face of the earth with technology, transportation, and so much more. As we build on the past, there is exponential growth in our expansion. Are we, as humans, creating our reality? Or are we discovering it? Could we be creating it AND discovering it?

My head started spinning thinking about all of this.

Topaz decided to grab another book and open it up. Out popped a quote by Tom Robbins:

"Curiosity, especially intellectual inquisitiveness, is what separates the truly alive from those who are merely going through the motions."

Topaz and I looked at one another, surprised to be seeing a quote by our all-time favorite author. Topaz and I started laughing upon receiving this quote by Tom, noting the synchronicity. Topaz is a huge fan of Tom, and she has lent me many a book by him. Ironically enough, Tom Robbins and Terence McKenna were good friends. Somehow it felt like they were both with us right now, in the Labyrinth Library, guiding us along on our journey.

Blaise added to Tom's words of wisdom:

"And while many, if not most, may just merely be going through the motions, it is the curious few that plant the seeds for the future. Those with the bold, abnormal ideas are the ones that shift consciousness to the next level." He paused before continuing, "Yes, I am looking at you girls."

Topaz and Blaise stared at each other for a moment, both of their pineal eyes glowing. Topaz has a distinct freckle on her forehead, between her two eyes, placed in the same spot as her spirit dragon's parietal eye. When the two of them get fired up, there's no mistaking the gleam coming from the center of their foreheads.

All four of us looked at Blaise with an understanding. Deep down we knew that we weren't "normal." It was always hard for us to fit into the box society tried to put us in. It seemed we were always questioning, searching for something deeper, looking for The Answer. Don't get me wrong, there were often times I wondered what it would be like not to question so much. Surely, life would be easier to just live day by day, going through the motions, accepting what I was told, doing what society expected of me. But something inside of me wouldn't allow it. There was so much more for me to do and see. And the only way I could possibly live out my life was to follow that. Whatever it was that was calling me outside my zone of comfort, luring me into the unexplored, inviting me into the darkest deep, enticing me into the unknown, that was what I had to follow.

I know that it is my duty to help turn the dark into the light, not by ignoring it, but by facing it.

Kaj grabbed another book and flipped it open:

"As you continue your journey onward (and inward), you will find your tribe. While interacting with other conscious-driven beings, together, you will change the world."

I thought about this for a moment. It seemed to me that like-minded people were often difficult to come by. Though there are plenty of conscious-driven people working to make the world a better place, there are still so many that seem to be sleeping.

Blaise spoke up again, as if he was reading my thoughts, the parietal eye on his head lighting up as he shared his wisdom. "While not everyone is as woke as you babies, that is okay. Though at times it can be difficult, try not to judge. They are on this journey home, just like you are. Trust that the right souls will enter your life at the right time."

I understood exactly what Blaise was trying to tell us. Rather than scrutinize those who are seemingly less "awake" or "connected" as you are, having patience is key. At the end of the day, we are all here together, learning from one another, growing, expanding, and shifting things further. Just because someone may not be at the same level of understanding as you are, doesn't mean they aren't working towards it. And it is up to YOU to continue questioning and pushing the limits.

The fiery green dragon continued with what he was saying, his third eye still shining brightly. "And girls, don't ever let your 'wokeness' trick you into thinking you are all-knowing, because you're not. There are plenty of enlightened beings who could teach you a thing or two and put you right back in your place should you let your ego get the best of you."

Once again, Blaise was right. Like he said, we are all on this journey together, teaching each other and guiding one another home. There is always more to learn.

Topaz opened the book she was holding to a different page. Another Tom Robbins quote spoke to us:

"Our great human adventure is the evolution of con-sciousness. We are in this life to enlarge the soul, liberate the spirit, and light up the brain."

My sisters and I looked at one another and somehow knew that we were on this journey for a reason. We were being shown things that would shift our perspective and take us to the next level. We put the books we were holding back on the shelves and continued walking.

I started to wonder, were we choosing the books off the shelves, or were the books choosing us?

Either way, I felt lucky to be here, now, in this inter-connected network of ideas. I expressed this to my sisters, grateful for where I was. Somehow, I felt as if all of this was important.

As we followed the winding walls of the Labyrinth Library, we could tell we were nearing the center. When we finally made it to the innermost point, we were mesmerized by what we saw awaiting us.

Centered in the middle of the library was a flower, floating in the air. It was glowing and it radiated so many different colors I had never seen before. I noticed the flower had four petals.

Not quite sure what to do, my sisters and I each walked over to the shelves surrounding us and chose a book. We each brought our books back to the center, where we surrounded the flower.

Bayou opened up her book first. Words popped out, offering guidance:

"When you are ready, each of you are to reach in and take one of the four petals from the flower. With this journey, you need to trust that you will be taken where you need to go and shown what you need to be shown."

Bayou closed her book. Kaj opened her book next. Not surprisingly, we were met with another reassuring quote by Terence:

"Nature loves courage. You make the commitment and nature will respond to that commitment by removing impossible obstacles. Dream the impossible dream and the world will not grind you under, it will lift you up. This is the trick. This is what all these teachers and philosophers who really counted, who really touched the alchemical gold, this is what they understood. This is the shamanic dance in the waterfall. This is how magic is done. By hurling yourself into the abyss and discovering it's a feather bed."

I could feel that we were just about ready for what was next. I opened my book to a spell to send us off:

"When you seek The Answer,
Life shows you a way.
In the search for truth,
All is play.

You may get distracted,
And that is okay.
It's the journey that shows you,
Answers come when you stray.

Things won't always be easy,
But come what may.
Follow your heart,
And say all you should say.

Know The Answer will come,
As you continue to pray.
The Time is Now.
Today is the day."

The four of us then proceeded to reach in, all at the same time, for the luminous flower. Just before we each grabbed our petals, Topaz realized she was the only one who hadn't opened up her book. She flipped it open just as our hands touched the radiant plant. The final words came from Tom Robbins. As we faded into the next chapter, we heard, "minds were made for blowing."

CHAPTER 15

FATE AND CHANCE

As soon as my fingers touched the gleaming plant, I started to feel myself drift away. I found myself in a sphere where technology and nature danced. I walked through a kingdom of duality. As I got oriented, I found my sisters beside me. It felt like we were in a dream world. We walked through a domain where towering buildings extended far up into the clouds, spacecrafts zoomed in and out of our scope of vision, rivers flowed like veins between otherworldly constructs, mountains looked over us from the distance, and the sky changed colors before our eyes.

We kept walking, taking in everything we could. It's like this world was the perfect mix of spontaneity and organization. Colorful patterns found a home on the walls of clean, modern buildings. Plants crept their way inside, outside, and all around the architecture. The wild mixed with the orderly in such a way that everything made so much sense, and no sense at all.

Even though there was so much going on, everything flowed. As we walked on a path that bled into endless other paths, a door with a sign that said FATE / CHANCE on it caught my eye. I stopped in front of it and asked my sisters if we should enter. They said yes. What would happen should they have said no?

I opened the door. The room was dark but the ceiling windows let in beams of falling light. There were beings on both sides of the room. The beings didn't have physical bodies. They were more like energies. I could sense a strong feminine energy from one and a strong masculine energy from the other.

They both gave us friendly welcomes. "What brings you here?" inquired the Feminine.

"I'm not sure," I spoke. "The sign on the door caught my eye as we were passing by and we decided to enter."

"You happened to be walking down this path by chance," started the Masculine.

"But you found yourself here by fate," continued the Feminine.

"Hmmm," I wondered.

Opposite the door we entered, on the other side of the room, was another door.

"Where does that lead?" I asked, pointing to the door.

Something about the door intrigued me. I started to walk closer to the door, drawn to whatever lie behind it. The Feminine encouraged me to open the door to find out. But when I went to turn the handle, I found the door was locked. I pulled at it a couple times, but couldn't get it to open.

"Looks like we're locked out," said the Masculine. "Do you have the key?" he asked the Feminine.

The Feminine searched around but couldn't seem to find it.

We decided to help them out by scanning the premises. We searched the rocky ground for anything that looked remotely like a key. We didn't find anything.

"Well, I guess it wasn't meant to be," I thought to myself.

Just as we were about to give up, Topaz tripped over a large, smooth, shiny stone. As she fell over on to her knees, the stone she tripped on tumbled with her foot, uncovering a silver key that was unmistakably what we were searching for.

I walked over to Topaz to make sure she was fine, and then took the key in my hand, showing it to the Masculine and the Feminine.

"It seems to me Topaz tripped by chance," started the Feminine.

"But it's by fate that we've uncovered the key," continued the Masculine, finishing the Feminine's sentence.

I walked over to the door, holding the precious key.

I looked to the two energies, asking for the go ahead to unlock the door.

Guiding me, the Feminine said "You've got the key..."

"Now why don't you see if it fits," said the Masculine.

I placed the key in the hole, and slowly turned it.

CHAPTER 16

TRANSFORMATION

When the door opened, we were hit with a blast of air. It was hot and then it was cold. The room whirled with extreme temperatures from arctic ice to desert heat.

The Masculine and the Feminine guided us through the room of hot and cold. We could feel the extremes, but we could also feel everything in between. As we shivered and sweat, the two energies led us to the next door.

We opened it and walked into a room of past and future. We could see it all. The past and the future came together, now. We were in the present moment. But as we walked on down to the next door, it seemed the present moment, though in and of itself was constant, was ever changing.

The Masculine and Feminine opened the following door of constant and change.

And so on and so forth, these two opposite energies led us down the path of duality, opening door after door.

We went into a room of day and night where the sun and the moon danced in their ever-glorious rotation. We walked through a room of 1's and 0's, where numbers whirled through the air. And then we walked into a room of science and religion, where the explainable blended with the unexplainable.

The Masculine and the Feminine explained that all these rooms of opposites were actually a part of the same ONE thing.

"There is truth in the light," said the Masculine.

"And there is truth in the dark," said the Feminine.

"The problem is, people often confuse yes as right, and no as wrong for example," said the Masculine.

"You see, it's never all fate, or all chance for that matter," started the Feminine. "It's the yes's and the no's, the day and the night, the 1's and the 0's, the past and the future, and so on and so forth, that encompass The Mystery. It's all of these opposing forces that make up the same one thing."

As we stood in the room of science and religion, I thought about all the people that are so sure that science is the answer, and all the others that believe religion is the answer.

The Masculine and the Feminine looked at me, seeing my thoughts, before telling me, "You see science and religion alike are barriers. Yes, they each have their truths, but they aren't IT. And in many ways, they block you from reaching IT. Especially when taken too seriously."

I started to understand.

We walked into the next room of creation and destruction. This was the first room we entered that didn't have a door on the other side.

"Is this the end?" I wondered. "On second thought, maybe this is the beginning…" I pondered.

The Masculine and Feminine energies let us know that this is where they would be leaving us.

But before they left, we stopped them. "Wait, we have to ask you something before you leave."

My sisters and I were all wondering the same thing. Maybe these two energies could give us insight into what we were seeking.

"Do you happen to know The Answer to The Question?"

There was grace in the way these two energies interacted.

The Feminine said, with what could be interpreted as a smile, "Know that you'll never really know."

The Masculine continued, "And know that you already know."

Just like that, the two energies vanished into midair.

The four of us were left in this final room of creation and destruction, wondering what to do next.

As deaths and births twisted around us, we started to understand the Oneness that the Masculine and Feminine were trying to convey to us. We realized that death and birth were one and the same. From destruction comes creation.

Every ending is a beginning. It's all one!

Unsure of what to do, we decided it was time for a spell. We had started to realize that on our voyage through Another Here, we were encountering situations in which we would each need to call upon our elements. Kaj helped us with her element of earth in the Underground. Now it was Topaz's turn.

Because Topaz is the element of fire, it seemed fitting we call upon her now to invoke the spirit. The element of fire itself represents destruction, creation, and transformation.

It was spell time.

The four of us stood together, about to speak our spell, when suddenly, the Masculine and the Feminine reappeared.

Apparently, they were here to help us with our spell.

The Masculine started:

"There's a time to give, and a time to take.
There's a time to sleep, and a time to wake.
While at times you'll be still, and at times you will shake,
Know, from this to that, is all for your sake."

The Feminine continued:

"Out of the dark, comes the light.
With time, day turns to night.
One side may be black, the other side white.
But it's the colors in between, that makes things bright."

They looked to me.
I started:

"From 0 to 1, there's infinite potential.
The Mystery itself, is exponential.

Know what is optional, and what is essential.
In this ever-changing world, you're influential."

Kaj spoke next:

"It's hot, then it's cold.
You're young, then you're old.
One moment you'll be shy, the next you'll be bold.
But from here to there, a story is being told."

Bayou continued:

"As summer turns to fall, and winter turns to spring,
It's the change in the air that makes your heart sing.
While you never know, what change will bring,
Something about it, is promising."

Now it was Topaz's turn. We knew that her final verse would propel us into whatever was to come. We closed our eyes and held on for the ride.

She spoke:

"From creation to destruction, and destruction to creation,
It's all about expanding, and gaining information.
It's as much despair, as it is elation.
This is the process, of TRANSFORMATION."

WATER

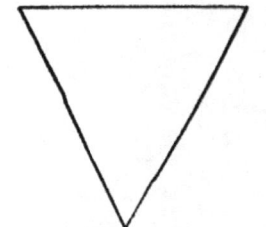

CHAPTER 17

MATRIX

The four of us found ourselves on a little island filled with colorful flowers, towering palm trees, and lush vegetation, surrounded by crystal clear water. The sky was bright blue and wispy white clouds danced around the beaming sun.

"Wow, where are we?" asked Bayou.

None of us knew, but wherever it was, it was beyond magical.

We decided to explore. We were curious how big the island was so we decided to walk along the shore for a while. We used a big red flower to mark our starting point. From there, we started to walk, our gazes drifting between the endless sparkling waters to our right and the dense green jungle to our left. We kept walking for what felt like a long time. The sun was beaming down on us and we started to get tired. After a while, we decided to sit down on the sand, admiring the sparkling, blue waters that seemed to never end.

"This place is paradise," said Bayou.

We were all thinking the same thing. But there was something else looming in all of our heads that wasn't so pleasant.

As beautiful as the island was, none of us were sure how we were going to get off of it. From any point on the shore of the island, for as far as our eyes could see, was just endless water.

"Now what?" asked Topaz.

Just as we were pondering what to do next, not really sure if we should continue along the shore or figure out a better plan, a giant blue butterfly fluttered up above us, headed inward toward the jungle. The four of us were mesmerized by the stunning beauty who seemed to effortlessly float through the air, off to wherever it was going.

We got up to get a better look at it, following close behind the majestic butterfly, as it led us to where the jungle began. Without further thought, we headed in. As we pushed our way through overgrown trees and bushes, we noticed all kinds of wild critters we had never seen before. Colorful insects crawled in and around big green leaves, giant bright butterflies fluttered through the trees above us, and cute little furry creatures climbed from branch to branch as we went deeper and deeper into the island.

The deeper we went, the darker it got, as the jungle around and above us seemed to grow denser and denser. It seemed like we were walking for a while and we started getting nervous that we wouldn't be able to find our way out.

"Where are we going?" asked Kaj.

"Maybe we should turn around," said Topaz.

"Yea, I think we're lost," said Bayou.

I was frustrated. I didn't know what to do. At this point it seemed like we were never getting home. And after everything we'd been through, we still didn't have The Answer to The Question. Why were we being taken to so many places if nobody could help us find The Answer? We sure got ourselves into a mess this time… I stood there, looking in every direction, trying to figure out which way to go. Nothing made sense. Everything looked the same. How deep into the jungle were we? How deep did it go? I was so disoriented and I started getting really nervous. As my three sisters stared at me, I looked back at them, waiting for some inspiration to come to me, when something behind them caught my eye.

I brought my hand over my mouth, trying not to let out a scream. My face must have had a look of horror mixed with awe as I stared at what was up in the tree behind them. The girls immediately turned around upon seeing my reaction. Wondering what had caught my eye, there was no mistaking what I was staring at as my sisters all turned around to see a giant snake slithering down a big tree, headed in our direction.

We all took a step back upon seeing the snake move from the tree to the ground, but as the snake slithered closer and closer, we stood there, mesmerized.

It was right up at our feet when it started communicating to us. We were shocked when the snake came over in a friendly manner to offer us some guidance.

"You look lost," said the snake.

"Yea, we don't really know where we are," said Bayou.

"Well, do you know where you're going?" asked the snake.

We all kind of just shook our heads.

"Well, that's the problem," said the snake. "Why don't you decide where you want to go? There are endless possibilities, you know."

We didn't really know what our options were. It didn't seem like there was much on the island. Endless possibilities?

"I'm going to meet up with a friend," said the snake. "You are welcome to join."

As he turned around and started to slither away, we decided to follow him.

As we walked beside him, he finally introduced himself. He told us his name was Matrix.

CHAPTER 18

PARADISE ISLAND

"May I ask, what are four young girls doing on Paradise Island?" inquired Matrix.

"I don't know. I think we ended up here by accident," I told him.

"We came to Another Here by casting a spell," said Kaj.

"We were looking for The Answer to The Question," said Topaz.

"But now we are just trying to get home," continued Bayou.

"I see," said Matrix. "Well, I may be bold in my statement, but I don't think you girls ended up here by accident. I think that you girls manifested all of this. ALL of your decisions have led you to the here and now."

"When you said that there were endless possibilities earlier, what did you mean by that?" I asked.

"There are always endless possibilities," said Matrix. "From any given moment, there are endless possibilities."

We walked in silence for a few moments before Matrix continued.

"Let's start at the beginning, when anything is possible. Imagine a blank canvas or a book with nothing yet written. You can create an infinite number of things from this starting point. The key is knowing that it is entirely up to you."

We let that sink in before Matrix added to what he was saying.

"Now imagine that every single second, life is both destroyed and created, because, well it is. From this very moment on, anything you can imagine, down to your wildest dreams, is possible. That's not to say that just because you want something, you will get it that easily. The more complex something is, the more time and energy it will take to come to fruition. Everything is manifested for a reason. Everything has a purpose. And EVERYTHING is tied to the Source. That means every single thing is connected. When you realize this, you stop living in fear, because you realize that what is good for you, is good for all, and what is good for all, is good for you. For that reason, what is meant for you, will always be yours."

I wondered if what Matrix was saying was true. Maybe we really did manifest all this. "So, everything in the history of everything has led up to this very moment. But why?" I asked Matrix.

"You are where you are and it is what it is," was all Matrix said.

I wasn't completely satisfied with Matrix's answer, but we kept on walking and I didn't push it.

The jungle seemed to hold so many wonders. Everything was so alive. I could feel the trees moving and breathing as I watched light and shadows form patterns all around me. As we followed Matrix deeper and deeper, I got this strange feeling that whatever it was we were doing was important. In that moment, I felt as if we were making history. If everything had led up to this very moment, this moment was everything. I realized that you have to appreciate where you are now, because wherever you are in this very moment, is an important part of the story.

"Did you say this island is called Paradise Island?" asked Bayou.

"That's what I call it," said Matrix. "As you live in love, you realize that paradise is always here. That's why I call this island Paradise Island. Paradise is no more in your head than hell is. It's just a matter of realizing it. But just look around! How can you not think this is paradise?!"

Matrix was right, the island was wonderful. But so many other places were equally sublime. I had traveled all over the world, voyaging from country to country, visiting remote beaches, enchanting cities, striking mountains, and cozy villages. And what I had realized along the way was that every single place has its charm. Paradise is more a state of mind than anything else. You can be on a beautiful beach and feel anxious because you are thinking about something else, and the beach, as beautiful as it may be, won't feel like paradise. And the opposite is also true. You can be in a less than picturesque place, but be content with where you are, realizing it's all paradise if you think it is. I got a flashback to my dad sitting out in our yard at home, feeding the birds and looking out over the lake. I remembered him saying, "It doesn't get any better than this. It might be just as good, but it doesn't get better." He was right! Paradise is your appreciation of the here and now, realizing that now is all there is. That doesn't mean you shouldn't strive for more and get excited about what the future holds, but appreciating wherever you are is key.

We kept walking and eventually it got darker and darker as day turned to night. Finally, we reached an area where the jungle opened up. I could see the sliver of a new moon shining above, unimpeded by any surrounding trees, stars twinkling around it, reflected in a lagoon where the water sparkled like the millions of stars above it. We couldn't believe how magical everything looked. Matrix laughed as he looked at the four of us, inflamed by the beauty of our surroundings.

We were giddy with excitement, moving closer to the enchanting lagoon, wanting nothing more than to bathe in its alluring waters, when something in the water caught our attention and made us stop in our tracks.

Matrix paid no attention to our shock as he slithered onward, eventually reaching the edge of the lagoon, where he greeted his awaited friend with a spirited kiss.

CHAPTER 19

THE MERMAID

Matrix's friend embraced us with a warm smile as she waved and introduced herself as Annala. All the while, Matrix was slithering up and down her arms, playing between her fingers, dancing around her upper body in a way that seemed unnoticed by Annala. My sisters and I moved in closer to make sure our eyes weren't playing tricks on us. It was dark out and the only light we had was a slice of the glowing moon and the surrounding stars. But upon reaching the lagoon, there was no doubt in our minds that Annala was exactly what we thought she was, a mermaid.

We had never met a mermaid before, let alone, known they even existed, so imagine our surprise when we encountered one in the middle of Paradise Island.

Annala splashed around the lagoon with Matrix coiled around her neck, examining us with a wondrous look in her eyes.

We introduced ourselves and explained to her (as much as we could) about how we ended up here. None of it seemed to phase her.

Annala told us that she had traveled far and wide and had encountered many situations equally strange, if not stranger, than meeting four witches in the jungle.

"How did you know that we're witches?" Bayou asked.

"A witch can see a witch," Annala replied. "Plus, Matrix told me."

"You're a witch too?" asked Kaj.

"I'm as much a witch, as you girls are mermaids."

We were unsure what Annala meant by that. She could see the skeptical looks on our faces and she laughed at us in a friendly manner before adding, "Is it that you don't believe I'm a witch? Or is it that you don't believe you are mermaids?"

"More so the latter," I told her, assuming my sisters would agree.

"I see. Well, would you girls like to tap into your mermaid power, just to see what it's like?" asked Annala.

As kids, my sisters and I would always pretend we were mermaids while splashing around in the pool, playing with our make-believe dolphin friends.

I think Annala knew what our response would be before she even asked the question. She told us that there was somewhere she wanted to take us and that having a fin over feet would get us there much more efficiently.

We weren't sure how our feet could magically transform into fins, but Annala reminded us that we were witches and we had more power than we realized.

"There's a simple spell I know of that could help you girls out," Annala told us. "Bayou, you are the element of water. You may not realize it, but generations of water witches live on through you now. Their ancient wisdom swims through your DNA. It's time for you to access it."

Annala motioned for Bayou to join her in the water. Bayou coyly dipped her toes into the magical lagoon and then slowly moved in deeper as the water enveloped her ankles and then her knees and then her waist. Annala said "repeat after me," as she recited the simple spell she had mentioned before. Bayou did as she was told.

> *"I call upon the water witches,*
> *For you know how to guide me now.*
> *I offer you my feet,*
> *If a fin you will endow."*

Bayou repeated the words but nothing happened. We all stood there, staring at Annala in a way that she might have read as "I told you so," affirming our belief that we couldn't possibly be mermaids.

But Annala paid us no attention and said, "Good, now you know the spell. Next, all you have to do is close your eyes, repeat the spell three times, and genuinely ask with your heart as much as your words, for what you want."

Bayou laughed a little nervously before saying, "Okay, here goes nothing!" She closed her eyes gently and repeated:

"I call upon the water witches,
For you know how to guide me now.
I offer you my feet,
If a fin you will endow.

I call upon the water witches,
For you know how to guide me now.
I offer you my feet,
If a fin you will endow."

She paused for a moment before she said it a third time, slowly.

"I call upon the water witches,
For you know how to guide me now.
I offer you my feet,
If a fin you will endowwwwww!!"

Her voice became higher pitched on her final words as she felt the transformation happening. All of us were astonished as we watched Bayou turn into a mermaid right before our eyes!

"Wow, this is so cool!!" said Bayou as she splashed around in the lagoon, enamored with her new fin.

Annala just smiled as she looked over at the three of us and said, "who's next?"

CHAPTER 20

THE COSMIC EXPLORER

One by one, we all went from having feet to fins. It was invigorating, swimming around the lagoon, diving deep into the sparkling waters, playing with our new shiny tails. Each one of us had a slightly different hue to our scaly bottoms. Mine was a blend of pink, blue and yellow pastels, each scale shimmering iridescent colors from different angles. Bayou's was a silvery white that glistened with the light of the moon. Topaz's tail was a shiny gold with undertones of regal purple. And Kaj's was olive green with a glossy caramel finish that gave it a lustrous glow.

Annala laughed as she watched the four of us playing with our tails, flapping around, and splashing each other. She let us play for a little while before she told us that if we were ready, there was somewhere she wanted to take us.

"Before we leave, I want to give you a few tips since you girls are new to all this," Annala began. "First of all, I don't know if you have noticed, but you are unable to breathe underwater. That being said, you will still be able to hold your breath for MUCH longer than you could as a mere human. Our journey underwater won't be anything you girls can't handle, but I suggest taking a deep breath before we begin. Secondly, when we begin our travels, I want you four to stay close to me. There will be many eye-catching things in the water world that you may have never seen and feel compelled to stop and observe. However, I don't want anyone getting lost down there. Like I said, I want us all to stay together. And third of all, have fun! It may be unnerving at first, being a sea creature, but gliding through the water is a blast. You girls will love it!"

To be honest, I was a little nervous at first. Annala didn't give us any clues as to where we were going and I was a little uncomfortable entering this realm that I had never experienced before. I think we all fear the unknown to some extent, but fear alone should never hold one back. I thought back to when Matrix asked us where we were going when we were lost in the jungle. We didn't know where we were going, but somehow, we knew we were headed in the right direction, lost as we were. You may not always know where you are going, but something deep inside of you knows whether you are following your path or not. Now, here we were, five witchy mermaids, headed to wherever Annala was taking us. And I had the utmost faith that we were being guided by the Source, through Annala, leading us back home.

"Okay babes, are you ready?!" Annala asked.

We all nodded our heads, with an equal amount of nervousness and excitement.

But first, we said goodbye to Matrix and thanked him for showing us a way. We weren't sure if we'd ever see him again but he assured us there was a chance that we would. He slithered from one sister to the next, giving us each an endearing kiss and a tight squeeze as he coiled around us. "There is nothing to fear," said Matrix as he tapped on my forehead with his tongue and said, "paradise is here."

Annala looked at us, making sure we were ready, before saying, "take a deep breath in, and follow me."

We all took in as much air as we could before we headed into the depths of the water. At first, I was a little bit panicky, holding my breath and trying to keep my eyes on the silvery fin of Bayou in front of me. The water was dark, as night was still upon us. However, after a few minutes, I started to notice lights in the water, making it much easier to see. I realized that we were surrounded by bioluminescent organisms in the water. It was such a magical sight, swimming through these glowing creatures, lighting the way for us. My tension started to ease and I began to enjoy myself. My sisters and I all looked at one another, pointing to the lights around us, amazed. Unbeknownst to us, we were able to communicate underwater, not through actual words, but with a language we didn't even know we had access to. Annala told us that she likes to call the bioluminescent plankton "little light fairies." She told us that the fairies would always be there to guide us when we needed them, especially in the darkest of times.

We followed Annala and the light fairies through underwater cave systems that seemed like a never-ending maze until we finally reached the vast open ocean. We came up for air and looked back at Paradise Island that was now a little way in the distance. I smiled as I looked up at the starry sky, at peace with where I was.

Annala motioned for us to follow her back underwater. Now, with much more space to play, the five of us weaved in and around each other, dancing like sirens of the sea. Before long, we were joined by a pod of dolphins that were clicking so loud it was almost deafening. The dolphins were so full of life it made me want to cry. I started to get really emotional as I connected to these creatures that were so majestic. I didn't know whether I was crying out of happiness or sadness. Annala looked at me, wondering what was going on in my head and I told her I wasn't quite sure. I didn't know why I was so emotional. I just was.

I felt so much love for these creatures that were playing beside me, happy and free. But it made me think of the unlucky creatures who don't have that freedom. I thought about the dolphins captured or born into amusement parks or sea aquariums. "Why?" I thought. "Why are some creatures born into lives of freedom and others into lives of enslavement?" My tears came flooding out more and more. "How can anyone possibly think it is okay to take another living creature, one that's meant to swim through vast oceans, and put it in a tiny tank, so that people can look at it?"

Annala listened to my thoughts and looked at me with an expression of understanding. My sisters listened to my thoughts as well and before long we were all tearing up, adding salt water to the endless sea. All four of us are equally emotional when it comes to animal rights. I don't know why we were so sensitive in that moment, but the four of us couldn't stop crying.

Luckily, Annala was there to console us. "It is evident that you girls care immensely about life," she said. "Your concern for the life of ALL creatures has driven you to where you are today. Yes, there are many injustices that are still taking place, but you are here to change that. That is a part of your calling. Believe it or not, we are at the highest level of consciousness to ever have been. But if you start from this point in time, looking forward, we are currently at the lowest level of consciousness. We are living in a backwards time, but most will only realize that in the future. Things are moving to higher and higher levels and it is your responsibility to keep raising those levels. You are here to push things forward. We are getting closer and closer to The Truth."

My sisters and I nodded in agreement. We knew Annala was right.

"Now wipe away your tears," said Annala "and keep moving forward. Never stop fighting against those injustices, but try to see the light as well. There is so much good and so much beauty." She gave us all a big hug and said, "I love you girls."

We did as she said and wiped away the tears and started to laugh at all of our emotional outbursts. Crying feels so good sometimes though.

Annala told us we weren't too far from our destination. We followed her for a little while longer until she stopped and told us we were finally at our spot. I didn't see anything around us until I looked up and noticed something floating above our heads in the water. Annala had us follow her to the surface where a boat awaited us.

Inside the boat sat a man with long dark hair, the ends reaching down into the water. I noticed that on the side of the boat, with silvery, polychromatic letters, read the words "The Cosmic Explorer."

CHAPTER 21

AMPHIBIAN MAGIC

Annala introduced us to Varish, the captain of The Cosmic Explorer.

"Varish will guide you on the next leg of your journey," said Annala. "Oh, speaking of legs…"

Annala pointed to our fins and told us that our shiny tails would no longer serve us. Apparently, we'd be traveling by boat now.

We were all a little sad to say goodbye to our fins. Our time as mermaids was short-lived but I wondered if we could transform ourselves again, now that we knew the spell. Annala told us there was another simple spell that would give us back our feet. Just as before, she told us that it needed to be repeated three times. She recited the spell for us before giving us the go ahead to do it on our own. This time around the four of us recited it at the same time, eyes closed, bobbing in the water next to the boat.

"I no longer need my fin,
as I move from water to land.
In exchange for my scaly tail,
I ask for two feet to stand.

I no longer need my fin,
as I move from water to land.
In exchange for my scaly tail,
I ask for two feet to stand.

I no longer need my fin,
as I move from water to land.
In exchange for my scaly tail,
I ask for two feet to stand."

The transformation happened quickly and having feet again felt a little bit strange at first. I had started to get used to having a fin.

One by one, Varish helped lift us up out of the water and into The Cosmic Explorer. As we boarded the boat, I realized that the sun had started to rise. The bright pink and orange hues in the sky painted a magnificent picture.

Once we were all in the boat, we said goodbye to Annala who was still in the water. She wished us a safe trip and said she hoped to see us again soon. She blew us a kiss and smiled at Varish who began to row us off.

Soon enough, Annala became a spec in the distance, some far off character from a dream, another chapter in the story.

Varish was beyond excited to finally "meet" us, though he knew plenty about us already. He was animated, joyous and full of life. The sun beamed down on him as he rowed us, his smile illuminated by the rays of golden light, and in that moment, I had the utmost faith that he was taking us to exactly where we needed to go. At the start of our journey in Another Here, I was much more nervous and fearful about where we were and what was going on. I didn't always fully trust what was happening. But now, I had this strange feeling that the Universe had our backs. Somehow, I knew that we were being guided along on our journey. It was just a matter of tuning in.

Varish rowed us to an estuary, taking us upstream through the brackish water. As we moved further up the stream and away from the ocean, the environment started to change. The water was shaded by a bunch of different trees and plants, and various creatures waded through the shallow water. As we neared a big log, we all noticed something sunbathing on it. As we got closer, we realized it was a turtle, and not just any turtle, it was Bayou's turtle!

Bayou's turtle, who she had named Turtlenet as a kid for some strange reason, saw us in the boat as we approached. We still make fun of Bayou for giving him that name. Anyways, as soon as the boat was close enough for Turtlenet to make a safe leap, he hopped on board to join us. Bayou scooped him up and gave him a big kiss.

"Turtlenet!! What are you doing here?! I am so happy to see you!" Bayou exclaimed while embracing her little guy.

Turtlenet said hello to all of us, including Varish, who he seemed to know already.

Curious as to how Varish seemed to know about us, we asked if we had met him before. Varish informed us that we had indeed met, but not in a way that we would expect. Apparently, we came to him in a dream.

Bayou, tapping in to a dream she thought she had long forgotten, recalled having interacted with Varish as well. Somehow, we had all connected in the spirit realm, and now we were here together, floating on The Cosmic Explorer.

Varish told us that he used to travel by land, in a van fully equipped with a bed, a kitchen, and a magical medicine cabinet. His van was also home to his guitar, a bowl full of crystals, incense, some special books, decorative images of deities, and other random beautiful items he collected along the way. However, a long time ago, a young student of meditation told Varish that he foresaw Varish taking The Cosmic Explorer to the sea, traveling the world, teaching and guiding humanity everywhere he went. And now, here we were. The boat had everything Varish needed. Imagine the decked-out van, except on the water. The Cosmic Explorer had so much charm and my sisters and I had so much fun exploring the boat full of goodies. Kaj picked up his guitar and started to play a tune, Topaz poked through his bowl of crystals, Bayou lit some incense, while I combed through his book selection, drawn to a novel that immediately caught my attention, called "Annala Memoirs of a Mermaid."

As we floated up the river, I closed my eyes and smiled. I was so content with where I was, now.

"This is the ETERNAL NOW!" reiterated Varish as he read my thoughts, with a huge grin on his face and a contagious laugh that sent us all into merriment.

Though the now is ever-changing, it is the now that makes up EVERYTHING.

"You are the ONE infinite nature that is," said Varish. "Everyone in One."

Turtlenet looked at us and said "I am you and you are me."

Varish expanded on Turtlenet's statement by saying, "I am you, you are me, WE are the only thing that has ever been, ever was, and ever will be."

Off in the distance, I noticed some movement up on the banks of the water, though I couldn't tell what it was. As we neared the hopping movement, I saw what looked to be hundreds, maybe even thousands of froglike creatures jumping around. Varish pulled the boat to shore and told us we had arrived.

I couldn't tell if the hopping creatures were frogs, toads, or some amphibian yet to be discovered by scientists, but the croaks and ribbits emanating through the air were so loud!

Varish chuckled and asked if we were ready for some amphibian magic!

Before I even got both my feet out of the boat, I was startled by the unexpected slimy weight that found a place on my leg. I jumped back at first, frightened by the unforeseen amphibian that wanted to say hi. As soon as one hopped off of me, another was on me. The same thing was happening to my sisters. Amphibians were jumping on and off of us faster than we could count.

Varish told us not to be startled. He told us they were just getting to know us.

We followed Varish up away from the river, where he looked for a dry piece of land, amphibians hopping on and around us all the while.

When we found our spot, Varish laid out a couple of blankets on the ground to create a space for us. He burned some sage to clear the energy and said some prayers. He then told us that we were going to go on another journey, but this time we wouldn't all be together. He told us that each of our journeys would be personal to the individual embarking on it. This made us all a little bit nervous. We were separating from one another? How would we make it home, each one of us apart?

Varish listened to our worries and reassured us with his words, "all paths lead home." He looked at us with a confident smile and continued, "trust yourself."

An amphibian hopped on to the back of Turtlenet which made him retreat into his shell.

Varish told us that in order for us to embark on our journeys, we would each need to find our very own amphibian.

That request didn't seem hard considering we each had about five on us at all times. But Varish told us that not just any amphibian would do; it had to be the one that was meant

for us. Out of the thousands of hopping cold-blooded verte-
brates surrounding us, I wondered how I was supposed to find
the *one* that was meant for me. Varish told us not to worry.
He told us we would attract exactly the right one at exactly
the right time.

So, we sat there. And we waited. Tons of little guys hopped
on and off of me and each time I wondered if this could be
"the one." Every now and then, one would stay a little while
longer and I would pick him up and hold him in my hand
and think, "is it you?" But somehow, I knew it wasn't. Bayou
found one that stayed with her awhile. We all thought that
maybe she found her frog or toad or whatever these creatures
were. Topaz and Kaj went from amphibian to amphibian but
none of them stayed. Varish just sat there quietly, letting it all
happen. It seemed like forever that we were just sitting there.
Just when I was about to lose hope on finding my amphibian,
one hopped up on my knee as I sat there cross-legged. At
first, I was going to brush him off, but when I took a closer
look, something about him intrigued me. I picked him up and
stared at him awhile. He stared back at me. There was this
knowing between us. This was my amphibian.

I held him in my hand, but not in a grip. I just let him sit on my open palm, allowing him the freedom to hop away if he so wished. He stayed and waited with me while my sisters searched on for their amphibians. Bayou was shocked when her initial one hopped off, leaving her to wonder why he left. But soon enough, another appeared, and not just any, this was Bayou's amphibian. She laughed when she realized how foolish she was for being so quick to assume her first amphibian was the one meant for her. She could now clearly see THIS was the one. Topaz and Kaj found theirs as well, at almost the exact same time.

Now that we each had our amphibians, Varish told us it was time. Our unique amphibians were here to help us each unlock something deep within ourselves. He gave us step by step instructions for what was about to take place. After reciting a spell, we would kiss our amphibian, before being thrust into The Void.

Kiss our amphibian? I wondered if that's where the saying "sometimes you have to kiss a lot of frogs before you find your prince" came from. But what I wondered about even more was what he meant by "The Void."

Varish told us that what we were about to experience would be the closest thing to death we had ever felt, though he told us not to fear, we would be just fine. And when we returned home, we would be awakened to a whole new state of being.

I knew that what was about to occur was extremely important, not only for myself, but for EVERYTHING.

Nervous as I was, I knew this was an essential part of the journey.

Varish reminded us that we were goddesses. "Rise up my sisters. The Goddess has returned."

He added some more words of wisdom when he said, "there is a place within the heart that transcends all physical dimensions."

My sisters and I smiled at Varish, amphibians in hand, ready to do some magic.

I had absolutely no idea what to expect, and there is absolutely no way I could have ever understood where I would be going. While I may have had some sort of intellectual understanding of what would be occurring, until I actually experienced it, I wouldn't totally understand it. Sometimes, something has to be *felt*.

We sat in a circle, the four of us with our amphibians, Varish beside us, and Turtlenet in the center. Turtlenet would guide us with the spell.

Before we began, Varish looked at each one of us and said,

"There is but ONE infinite. It alone exists. If there were multiple infinites, neither would be truly infinite. For each would be a limit upon itself, a boundary where this one is and the other is not. Infinite knows no such boundary. It is infinite, it has no boundaries, there is no place it is not. Meaning you are this infinite. You are the ONE."

He stopped before concluding, "Thank you for being such a radiant reflection of this Divine creation."

The four of us smiled, feeling the oneness.

Then, Turtlenet started the spell:

"My witches sublime,
I believe it is time,
to face something never revealed before.

You've accessed the key,
to be able to see.
Now I ask you to open the door.

Don't worry my dears,
there's nothing to fear,
but your very own mind that you're here to explore.

As you delve into the void,
there's not a thing to avoid,
It is YOU that you cannot ignore.

So, pucker your lips,
To go on a trip,
and find out what you've got in store.

As you go deep,
Behold the secrets you keep.
You'll access The Answer, and maybe some more."

Apprehensively, I closed my eyes, held my amphibian up to my pursed lips, and gave him a kiss.

AIR

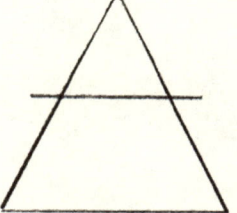

CHAPTER 22

THE ANSWER

As soon as my lips met my amphibian's lips, I was gone. I was immediately shooting through space, no longer in my body. It's hard to describe exactly where I went, though it felt like I was everywhere. I was a part of everything, literally, everything. If I could take a guess at what dying must feel like, I would guess it feels like that. I totally lost myself as I entered The Void. The Void was vast, expansive, and ever-changing. It was a place where ultimate reality is established. The Void was a place of nothingness from which everything emerges. It was life and death together as nothing and everything. It was the end and the beginning. It was as much the cosmos as it was a bar of chocolate, as much a cancer cell as it was a flower, as much a grasshopper as it was a bolt of lightning, as much a telephone as it was an alien. It was as much the tangible as it was the intangible, as much the conceivable as it was the inconceivable. There was no differentiation between this and that. Everything just *was*. I was in total union with the infinite, completely absorbed in all that is.

I felt an intense life force energy pulsing through me and all around me. It was overwhelming. I realized generative energy is at the base of EVERYTHING. I could *feel* it! I could *feel* it all. And it was this *feeling* more so than any intellectual understanding I thought I had, that gave me this *knowing*.

As I started to return to my physical body, I saw the constant movement, even in the stillness of a single object. I saw the ongoing dance happening between the tiniest of particles to the grandest of galaxies. Amongst the chaos of it all, was an incomprehensible organization. I found myself in this abyss where I felt everything from utter terror to extreme euphoria. Overwhelmed with emotion, I started to cry. The tears flooded down my cheeks, every single emotion pouring out of me. This very moment was EVERYTHING.

To be alive is the greatest miracle there is. How could it be that I ever doubted my very own divinity? I am everything that has ever been and everything to come. I am ALL. I AM.

And in that moment, I understood that I was crying because I had found The Answer to The Question. And I was laughing because I realized I had known it all along.

CHAPTER 23

AKPOBOME

I found myself in a dream-like land, where anything was possible. I woke up on a ship. The vessel was a mix of old, wooden architecture combined with a sleek, modern, galactic design. Unsure of where I was or where my sisters were, I made my way from the inside of the ship to the outside, where I was shocked when I looked out over the starboard side. Rather than floating on a big body of water, I was instead sailing through the air. I was a little frightened at first when I looked down and saw nothing but endless sky and clouds drifting around me. It seemed like I was in the middle of nowhere, lost in space, on a giant ship, coasting aimlessly through the heavens. But then, I noticed something off in the distance, a spec of blue, moving closer to me. As it came closer and closer, I realized it was a bird, and not just any bird, it was my bird, Soleil!

Soleil landed gracefully on my shoulder and I don't know if ever in my life I had been happier to see someone. I gave Soleil a kiss and a cuddle with the top of my head. I ran my hands through her feathers and told her how overjoyed I was at the sight of her. Soleil was excited to see me as well. It felt like forever since we had been together. It was as if I had been traveling through Another Here for a lifetime.

I asked Soleil if she had seen my sisters. "Don't worry, Aella, they are on their own journeys home now, just as you are. You will reunite again when the time is right," Soleil reassured me.

"Let me show you something!"

Soleil flew toward the front of the ship and I followed behind her, trying to keep up. The strong winds blew my hair in every direction. As I was removing my tangled hair from in front of my eyes, I was surprised when I saw that I was not the only one aboard the ship. Soleil landed on the shoulders of a young man that was adjusting the sails of the ship, focused on catching the wind, unaware of me moving towards him.

The strangely familiar man greeted Soleil with a smile as he tied off the ropes. "Hey there!" he said to Soleil, still unaware that I was watching. He stroked the feathers on Soleil's head as he said, "good to see you."

Soleil purred in contentment. The man looked like some sort of planetary pirate, sailing through space, with Soleil on his shoulder. I slowly made my way closer, fascinated. As soon as he saw me, he stopped and stared in perplexity.

Even though we had never met before, there was recognition as we looked into each other's eyes. We both started to laugh as we realized how ironic it was, meeting here, in this dreamy place up in the clouds, even though we had known each other forever. We hugged and Soleil hopped from his shoulder to mine as we embraced. He told me his name was Skyler and I told him my name was Aella.

"Where are we going?" I asked Skyler.

"Anywhere you want."

"Well, we've been trying to get home, my sisters and I. But now I'm not sure where they are."

"I'll take you home, if you want. But first, I'd like to show you something."

Curious about what Skyler wanted to show me, and not sure I was ready to go home just yet, I let him steer the way.

We sailed through the sky, floating through wispy clouds, vibrant atmospheric colors, and shooting stars. I felt so at home, soaring through the cosmos.

After a little while, I saw something up ahead in the distance. I couldn't tell what it was at first, but it looked like a big structure. I wondered what this place was, out here in the middle of space. As we neared it, I saw that the structure was a big castle, surrounded by clouds and sparkling lights.

"Wow, this place is so magical!" I said.

Skyler laughed as he steered the ship up to a floating dock and said, "It's yours, Aella."

We pulled up to the dock and a man approached with a big smile on his face. "How are you, Pilot?" he asked Skyler. "Good to see you again." He tied off the ropes to steady the ship to the dock.

The man, who told me his name was Ermir, took my hand to help lift me out of the ship as he nodded to me with a smile and said, "Welcome, Goddess."

Soleil, still on my shoulder, squawked loudly at the sight of this new person. I laughed at Soleil, knowing it always takes her a couple of moments to warm up to others. Ermir took a step back from my protective bird, smirking at the feisty creature.

I stepped out on to the glistening dock and followed Skyler and Ermir up to the castle. We were greeted at the front doors of the castle by a girl named Opal. She opened the doors for us and led us inside. The insides of the castle were like nothing I had ever seen before. Everything around me glimmered in colors I hadn't previously known existed. Opal was very warm and affable. She walked us through the castle around the wide, winding hallways, and then she stopped in front of a door and gave it a gentle knock. Out came another girl named Arya who had the biggest smile on her face as she greeted us. I could feel the warmth of Opal and Arya through the light in their eyes and their beaming grins. The two of them were beautiful, dressed elegantly in attire that looked primitive. They told me that they were taking me to meet Akpobome.

I followed behind Opal and Arya with Skyler and Ermir walking behind me and Soleil still on my shoulder. I looked back at Skyler, making sure he was still nearby, searching for the comfort in his eyes. He put his hand on my unoccupied shoulder and gave me a look that told me I was exactly where I was supposed to be in this moment. Then he gave Soleil a little pet on her back feathers to which she replied with a grunt and a quick snap toward his hand, obviously not wanting to be touched. We all started laughing. Soleil has such a funny personality. We reached a winding staircase. Opal and Arya moved aside to let me lead the way up. I stood there for a moment, taking everything in. There were beautiful gold curtains draped along the outside of the winding stairs. I stared at the intricate patterns on them. The drapes were embroidered with so many dazzling details. I closed my eyes and lifted my right foot to put it on the first step.

As I put my foot down on the initial step up, I heard "let Spirit guide you." I saw that there is so much happening beyond the scope of our understanding. And even though we may not be able to see Spirit or comprehend exactly what it is, following that guidance is essential. Spirit is in EVERYTHING. And everything is in YOU. Surrendering to Spirit is key. I opened my eyes and noticed more light creeping towards me as one of the golden drapes had fallen to the ground.

I tried to peer out over the edge of the staircase to see where the magnificent golden drape had gone. But it was nowhere to be seen, consumed by the cosmos.

I kept moving forward.

I realized there is nothing to fear. Heaven (and hell) are here. They are merely states of consciousness. It's all in your head. The whole world you live in comes from your head. Everything is your perception. And so, your life can be whatever you will it to be.

It's all for you. There's no need to worry- what's truly yours, will always be yours.

Through it all, you can't take anything too seriously. Play, create, and enjoy. It's all one big cinematic joke, and you're a fragment of it, living and acting out a part. The Enigma is an ironic, all-inclusive, poetic game. Once you realize this, there's nothing to do but laugh. I felt a smirk creep across my face.

With every step up the stairs, on my way to meet Akpobome, the lavish, golden curtains fell, one by one, letting in more light.

Every inch of the way up, I was having moments of enlightenment. I felt my third eye, that space on my forehead that held the force of my intuition. I was *seeing*, not with my two eyes, but with that eye that shows you something deeper. I was *understanding*. And beyond understanding, I was *knowing*. I felt the crown chakra above my head. I realized there was no end to the moments of enlightenment I would continue to have. Life is a process of waking up, an unveiling of truths. And these Universal Truths are beyond Time and Space.

I realized there is a mass spiritual awakening happening right now. We are at the highest level of consciousness to ever have been. As we move forward in time, it is up to us to keep shifting things to higher and higher levels.

As you begin to awaken, so does everything around you. It starts with you and ends with you. By healing yourself, you heal all. Self-love is everything.

I saw that everything is here for a reason, whether by chance or fate. Everything has a purpose.

I finally understood that being a witch has less to do with potions, spells, and rituals, (though these things may be helpful), and more to do with tapping into one's OWN power, in whatever way one chooses. Everything I had been seeking was within me all along. I had gone to Another Here, looking for something that was Here already. But for whatever reasons, I needed to be taken away to come right back home. What would be the fun of life if one was never to leave home? The things you learn while you're away…

I realized that I am the center of my own Universe, as every individual is. There once was a philosopher who defined God as an "infinite sphere, whose centre is everywhere and whose circumference is nowhere." I now understood exactly what that meant. My life revolves around me, as does each and every one of our lives.

But as a whole, we continue to evolve. Each one of us plays an intricate part. We are all ascending together, as ONE. Which is why YOU must live in your own light and truth for the benefit of all. Everyone (and everything) is a part of the same one thing.

As I reached the top, with the lights of heaven beaming down on me through the vast, uncovered windows, I realized that I am the writer of my own destiny. I saw that everything is NOW. I looked at the door in front of me, curious and excited about what lie ahead. I put my hand on the doorknob, ready to meet Akpobome. I looked back at Skyler one last time, wondering if he would accompany me into the room. "I'll wait for you on the other side of Here," he told me. I smiled, knowing I'd see him again.

I turned the knob and stepped into the light.

CHAPTER 24

WITCH SISTERS

Upon opening the door to meet Akpobome, I started laughing. I had been expecting to meet some great King or Queen, some highly important God, an all-knowing Creator. Instead, I met myself.

I saw myself in all forms. I was a unique piece of the puzzle, as was everything else. And this life was MY life. I realized that Akpobome simply meant "My Own Life."

I was the Creator, discovering myself.

I realized that I was a little, intricate, perfectly mathematical piece of The Mystery. Just the same as a cell in my body is a little, intricate, perfectly mathematical piece of my human form. That cell in my body may not be able to comprehend exactly what it is a part of, but it knows it has to follow its purpose for *me*. Because it *is* me. And that cell will do anything for me, because we are one and the same.

I saw that I was a part of something so much grander, of

which I was unable to even comprehend. But for that Mystery, I would do anything. And I trusted it would steer me in the right direction if only I listened.

I stopped for a moment and prayed.

"Help me,
Guide me.
I am here for you,
And I will do whatever you want me to do.
For you I will devote my life,
Because it is for you that I live.
You are me, and I am you."

I felt as if I had been initiated into something. I had this knowing, and I would be taking it back with me in my own life and journey. I was writing my own story, following my destiny.

All of a sudden, my life started flashing before me. I was getting glimpses of every experience that had brought me to this moment since the time I was born. I realized I was born into MY life for a reason. Every soul in my life served a purpose for me. And those closest to me were especially important.

Every single soul in my life reflected something back to me. I saw my parents. Each of them had taught me so much and helped shape who I was now. And with every interaction, they were continuing to shape me. Both my mom and my dad are such important people to me. I look up to them so much. And then I saw my sisters. Each one of my sisters is unique in her own way. And each one ultimately shows me something about myself.

I realized how lucky I was to be born into the family I was born into. My parents and my sisters are my closest friends. And I knew that as a unit, we had so much potential. All the people placed in each one of our lives serves a purpose to help us grow and evolve. And in turn, they evolve too. Whether these people be family, friends, or even just those random souls that seem to enter your life at the most spontaneous of times, they are here to show you something. And this process of transformation encompasses EVERYTHING!

Despite the fact that some may view their circumstances as seemingly "bad" or more difficult, it's all a lesson. It's just a matter of being able to take a step back in order to see more clearly. Whatever you are feeling is here to show you something about yourself. It's all perspective. What may seem like a curse, may actually be a blessing. The challenges we all face are here to propel us to the next level.

I started to get excited about my life and what lie ahead. I knew that so much more was going to happen and I felt blessed to have some amazing beings by my side through it all. Though I knew I would face more challenges to come, somehow, something told me everything was going to be okay. I wondered where my sisters were in that moment. I couldn't wait to tell them about my reunion with Soleil and meeting Skyler. Oh, and Akpobome too! And I couldn't wait to hear everything they had to share about their personal journeys.

And then Skyler appeared. I was so happy to see him. He told me that it was time for me to go home. I was excited to be back home with my family and the life I knew, but I had a sadness too.

"When will I see you again?" I asked Skyler.

"I will come to you, when the time is right," Skyler replied. "But know that I am with you all along."

As Skyler said this, I realized that he had been with me all along already. Though we had seemingly just "met," I felt as if I had known him forever. And in that moment, I realized the same held true for everyone in my life. I thought about my sisters and how they always were and always will be a part of me. No matter how much time and how much space may separate souls, they are never really apart.

As I stood there looking at Skyler, I noticed a pendant around his neck that I hadn't previously noticed. Hanging from the chain was a spiral. I put my hands up to it and held it, admiring it. I released it and smiled at him. And then I gave him a kiss.

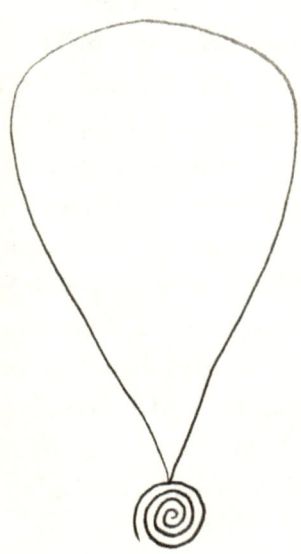

Skyler and I embraced in such a way in which we melted into one another.

I didn't want to let him go but I knew it was time for me to go home. And I knew that he would be with me, always, until we were to "meet" again.

"Are you ready to go home?" Skyler asked me.

I nodded my head yes.

Skyler told me that we would need to do a spell to send me off.

I knew exactly what to do.

I closed my eyes and started:

"Pondering The Question,
On a journey I went,
Looking for signs,
That were heaven-sent.

With my sisters by my side,
We found a way to circumvent,
Every obstacle in our course,
As we made our ascent.

Though there were times that were tough,
And there were hardships we underwent,
There was beauty and freedom alike,
And we saw that Love is always prevalent.

I found answers to questions,
I didn't even seek with intent,
And I realized life shows you the way,
With every event.

It was when I stopped pursuing,
And found that I was content,
I was given The Answer,
Realizing what this all meant.

As I head back home,
I know that I have to represent,
All that there is,
So that we can grow and invent.

Every individual journey,
Is time well-spent,
For it's this spiraling path,
That shows you Home is present.

HERE

CHAPTER 25

HOME

When I opened my eyes, I was back in Kaj's room. My sisters were all beside me. We were sitting in a circle on her floor. We all looked at one another and immediately started laughing and crying.

"What just happened?!" exclaimed Kaj.

"What a trip!" said Topaz.

"We're back home?" asked Bayou.

"Have we been home all along?" I wondered.

We all decided to get up and walk around the house. We tiptoed past mom and dad's room but realized they weren't around.

"I wonder where mom and dad are…" said Bayou.

"What time is it?" asked Kaj.

"What day is it?" asked Topaz.

"Are we really here?" I wondered.

We walked downstairs and into the kitchen.

Bayou opened the back, sliding glass door and called us over to look at the glowing full moon. It felt like déjà vu.

We walked outside into the yard to get a better look. Soleil was sleeping on her perch, Turtlenet was out in the lake dreaming, Blaise was up in a tree silently snoring, and Sam was out in the dirt dormant.

We walked back inside and looked at one another, each of us trying to find the words to say, wondering what just happened.

We stood there silently for a few moments before Bayou broke the lull. I noticed her staring at my neck and I wondered what she was looking at. She pointed and said, "Aella, where'd you get that necklace?"

Unaware that I was even wearing a necklace, I touched my hand to my neck and looked down. What I found was a pendant with a spiral dangling from the chain.

I held it in my hand and I noticed a huge smile creep across my face.

Before I could find the words to begin to explain where I got the necklace, the front door opened, startling us all.

In walked mom, dad, and Richie.

"Hi girls! We're home!" mom called to us.

"The concert was amazing!" said Richie.

The three of them slowly made their way into the kitchen.

Mom and dad looked at us and asked,

"So, did you girls have a good night at Home?"

If only they knew...

My sisters and I all just smiled and said, "There's no place like Here."

The end...

Is the beginning.

ABOUT THE AUTHOR

Alanna Murphy is a young, enthusiastic writer with a degree in Communications from The University of Florida. In addition to *Witch Sisters*, she is also the author of *Annala Memoirs of a Mermaid*. Her writings draw upon the spiritual, touching on the journey of life and the lessons we learn along the way. She has traveled extensively and believes traveling is the best way to not only learn about the world but to also learn about oneself. Aside from her interests in writing and traveling, Alanna is also an artist. All the sketches included in this novel are Alanna's creations.